Contents

FOLK TALES

FROM THE

GARDEN

DONALD SMITH

ILLUSTRATED BY ANNALISA SALIS

The
History
Press

First published 2021

The History Press
97 St George's Place,
Cheltenham,
Gloucestershire,
GL50 3QB
www.thehistorypress.co.uk

British Library Cataloguing in Publication Data.
A catalogue record for this book is available from the British
Library.

ISBN 978 0 7509 9568 9

Typesetting and origination by Typo•glyphix, Burton-on-Trent
Printed and bound in Turkey by Imak

*For William, Esther and Roberta Houston, and
Willie O'Hara: my Irish storytellers*

Introduction

A Calendar
of Stories

Most of us encounter plants, birds, animals and insects in gardens or parks. *Folk Tales from the Garden* celebrates this relationship through the changing seasons, with stories that have been created over generations.

During any given year, or even month, we can experience an astonishing variety of weather in Britain and Ireland, along with a constantly shifting balance between daylight and dark. These changes generate dynamic patterns of growth, decay and renewal. Life is always on the move, sometimes visibly and sometimes hidden from view.

These cycles are, of course, 'out there' in the natural world, but we also experience them in daily emotions and perceptions. That is hardly surprising since human beings are part of nature, yet we often appear unaware of our intimate connection. Robert Burns, Scotland's national poet, described his connection with a field mouse whose home his plough had upturned as belonging to 'Nature's social union'.

My own garden sits on sloping ground below Arthur's Seat, which is a royal park in Edinburgh. The landscape and climate of central Scotland are similar to that of our southern uplands, northern England, the Midlands, much of Ireland and the Welsh Marches. By contrast, the Scottish Highlands and southern England have significantly different seasonal timings and natural habitats.

North of my small walled garden is a patchwork of enclosed gardens dating from medieval times to the eighteenth century, when Scots embraced the ideal of *rus in urbe*, or 'countryside in the town', as embodied in gardens. In my more immediate area, there is a mix of suburban gardens, including nineteenth-century villas and twentieth-century bungalows.

To the south and east lie what were once enclosed estates. Their woods and parklands still survive in places, alongside built-up areas of modern housing, industrial estates and sports grounds. The land is criss-crossed by streams, or burns, stretching towards Duddingston Loch and the Forth shore, though these are blocked due south by Craigmillar with its wooded hill and castle. The south-facing chateau-style formal garden there brought much needed consolation to Mary Queen of Scots. In earlier times, all the surrounding territory was a royal hunting ground for Scotland's medieval kings.

In different ways these gardens are a bridge between humans and nature. Each day, if I keep my senses alert, there is something different happening in my garden and across this wider environment. In addition to the seasonal changes, there are many people encouraging and sustaining natural diversity in the face of climate change. Alongside the private enclosed gardens there are community gardens, allotments and actively managed public green space.

Many storytellers, gardeners, poets and naturalists have inspired these pages – too many to name. But among the naturalists, I must mention David Stephen and Michael Chinery, whose books were prized childhood possessions, and the prolific all-rounders, Richard Mabey and Mark Cocker. The storytellers to whom I owe especial gratitude include tradition bearers Duncan Williamson and Ruth Tonge; fellow storyteller and gardener Grian Cutanda; literary masters Hans Christian Andersen, Rudyard Kipling and Beatrix Potter; anthologists Joseph Jacobs,

Norah Montgomerie, Jean Marsh, Vigen Gurion, who introduced me to the Armenian Apocrypha, and Italo Calvino, who so meticulously and modestly points the way to those who heard and transcribed the peasant storytellers of Italy. It has also been a special pleasure to collaborate again with Sardinian illustrator Annalisa Salis, who has over the years become one of Scottish storytelling's best friends.

My hope, of course, is that this book will encourage your own observations, memories, imaginings and creative interventions. Perhaps it is through our gardens – past, present and future – that we can make our peace with nature and repair the planet we have so foolishly tried to conquer and destroy.

JANUARY

January comes in dark, cloudy and damp. This began before Christmas, after a cold snap, fulfilling the gloomy prognostication – 'Green Yule makes a full kirkyard'. Flues abound and in far-off China a new virus gestates.

We are past the year's shortest day, but there is little sign, as yet, of any change in our northern latitudes, morning or evening. Oddly, short days mitigate against growth, yet all the other conditions are present. The vegetable bed still harbours turnips, winter cabbage, leeks and kale. Scottish winter gardens were once called 'kailyards', which came to signify all things homely, practical and parochial. The kailyard supplied soups and helped give flavour to slightly mouldy stored potatoes. But there is little impetus for warming broths when the temperature ranges between 6 and 12 degrees centigrade.

Some almond blossom shows prematurely, along with a few branches of flowering currant. Snowdrops appear in some locations and the crocuses are pushing through. The garden birds are active, though perhaps puzzled. Blue tits, sparrows, chaffinch, bullfinch, robin and wren can feed freely without depending on human supplies. There is fresh water aplenty. Each evening gossipy jackdaws gather over the higher roofs, ready at some mutually determined moment to fly to roost in the crags of Arthur's Seat. Has that departure time shifted a little later? A first clue perhaps to the barely discernible lengthening of light, still overshadowed by cloud.

The digging impulse has petered out, but I do tackle the nettles that cluster in an old turf bank at the foot of the vegetable beds. Presumably at some point the beds were extended; the turf was cut and stacked at one end. The nettles love this rough bank and have rooted in deep. However often I dig them out, they come back. Of course, the old kailyarders would have welcomed these sturdy native nettles for soup and curative infusions.

I feel the lack of frost like an ache or absence. I imagine weeds waking far too early in earth that should be asleep and dreaming. The compost bins are overflowing, neither freezing nor fermenting, to the naked eye at least. The worms look pallid and sluggish. I treat them tentatively to a small keg of beer that was opened but not finished at Hogmanay. They definitely liven up and catch the party spirit despite dreich days.

It is time to take advantage of this unexpected and slightly dreary lull. A long-postponed clearance of badly overgrown ivy down the garden boundary becomes possible. We have new neighbours with a baby, and they will want to start afresh with their garden, unencumbered by my accumulated ivy thickets, entangled as they are with some neglected shrubs.

There are at least three kinds of ivy in this unpremeditated and uncontrolled hedge. One variety is flowering, and its leaves have become less variegated and more pungent. It is a heavy, hidden scent, dark and mouldering, though not poisonous. The plant's latent energy seems to contain all the recessive strength of these unseasonable conditions when everything is on pause.

The plants range from thick-trunked bearers to trailing outriders, which then take root in their own right. Also in the mix are old briars, and Russian vines unwisely added at some haphazard juncture to ornament the boundary. All of this must go, to be replaced in early summer by climbing roses and small apple trees. That will provide colour and foliage of some kind all year round. I begin, armed with saw, shears and secateurs. But is this a long campaign rather than a single battle? Have I underestimated the scale of the task?

January begins traditionally with important rituals, such as Twelfth Night and Wassailing the apple trees while nourishing their roots with cider! As the month proceeds, Scotland prepares for Robert Burns Day on the 25th. In recent times, that natal feast of our national poet has become a week-long festival. Of course, we need winter festivals in the north from our New Year Hogmanay onwards. Burns becomes an excuse for recitations, dramas, toasts, music, song and haggis.

Haggis is a mix of oatmeal and offal cooked in a sheep's gut. In harder times it was an ideal way to use every part of older animals that had been killed for our winter survival. Even the sheep's head was used to add flavour to a winter vegetable soup – 'sheep's heid' broth. Haggis should be served with 'chappit [mashed] tatties' – potatoes from the winter store – and turnips – 'neips' – also mashed. These delicacies are neither light nor especially delicate, but they do evoke a hardy spirit of survival in which farm and garden play their complementary parts.

At one time, turnips and kale were vital staple foods, essential to humans and animals for winter survival. Now people can eat them with sentimental relish, or culinary incredulity. Robert Burns reminds us of the need to hang together even through warmer days, because harder times may return to challenge our solidarity and good fellowship.

Twelve Months

Once upon a time, not in your time or my time, but it was once upon a time – there was a king who had two daughters. There were five years between the girls. Now, the first princess, Annie, was as cheery and as lovely as the day was long. She was always kind and considerate to everyone she met. But her younger sister, Jezebella, the second princess, was grumpy, spoilt and lazy. She was always whingeing and moaning as if everyone and everything was conspiring to make her life a misery. She stayed in bed most of the day watching Netflix and sending nasty tweets to her so-called friends.

Now the queen was very jealous of the king's affection for her older daughter. She watched for every chance to slight Annie and make her look bad beside her younger sister, Jezebella. But it was almost impossible to do this, because the king was very loving to both girls, and besides, Annie was so nice that nastiness washed off her like water off a duck's back.

Then one time, a week before Christmas, there was hunger in a distant part of the king's lands. The weather had been terrible with deep frosts and blizzards of snow. The king, being a good king, set off immediately to help his people, leaving the queen in charge at home.

She did not act immediately but circled like a watchful snake homing in on her prey. 'Dear daughter,' she said to Annie, 'you know that the king is away from home. But I am sure that when he returns, he would like to taste some fresh blackberries.'

'That would be nice, mother, for sure,' Annie replied, 'but blackberries are out of season, especially in this cold weather. The garden is frozen over, even the walled fruit garden.'

'Nonsense, girl, have you no consideration for your own father? Sometimes I think you have no feelings for him at all, unlike your dear sister who is so affectionate towards her parents. Of course there are blackberries out in the forest. Here is a basket for you to fill with fresh fruit. Bring it home so that your father can enjoy the berries when he returns.'

The princess did not wholly recognise her sister in the queen's description, but she did not protest or complain. Instead, she wrapped up warmly and headed into the forest with the empty basket on her arm.

'That's the last we'll see of her,' thought the queen, gloating at the newfound power she had over the elder daughter now that her father was far from home.

But as Annie walked through the forest, the snow seemed to get deeper and deeper. You could hardly see the undergrowth where blackberries might grow, as it was all buried below mounds of white snow. Also, a fierce north wind was blowing through the bare branches, driving the falling flakes into her face. Darkness descended on the forest. The girl trudged on, but she was tiring and was about to give up and turn back when she saw what seemed like a glimmer of light ahead. 'Perhaps,' she thought, 'there is a woodcutter's cottage in this part of the forest.' Annie's step quickened and her courage rose.

As she drew towards the light it became stronger, and suddenly Annie was looking into a clearing amidst the trees. At its centre was a roaring log fire and round the fire sat a circle of little people huddled in rugs and shawls against the cold. The girl stopped, astonished at the sight.

'Come away in, lass, and welcome!' said a little old man with a long straggly beard and red woolly bonnet. 'Come and warm yourself up beside our fire.'

She went forward gladly. The wee men and women made room for her and soon she was sipping a hot fruity drink from a wooden beaker.

'Well,' said the little old man, who seemed to be some kind of king. 'What is a girl like you doing out in the forest on a night like this?' Twelve pairs of little twinkling eyes settled on Annie.

'My mother, the queen, sent me out to look for blackberries for my father,' she explained.

'Well, well, your mother, you say. Very queenly she must be. It's not the time for blackberries,' replied the little king kindly.

'I know. I can't find any berries in the garden or the forest.'

'Maybe we can help,' said the king, looking round the circle. 'October, would you be so kind?' He gestured towards a little old lady with curly white hair and cheerful russet cheeks like an autumn apple.

'Of course, my dear,' she said and gestured for the basket.

Someone beside Annie took the basket from her hands and passed it round the circle towards October, who then passed it on round. By the time it came back the basket was full to overflowing with blackberries. Annie could not believe her eyes.

'There, there,' said the wee king, 'are you warmer now? You'd best be off home as this night is not going to get any better.'

'Thank you,' gasped Annie. 'I don't know how to thank you.'

'No need,' said October, chuckling. 'When you're old like me, it just comes naturally.'

'But who are you?' hazarded Annie, turning back to the little old man in the red woolly bonnet.

'I'm December,' he chuckled in reply. 'A kind of Christmas king. And we are all earth helpers.'

So off Annie went with a swift, sure step, feeling the wind behind her, while even the snow seemed less deep. In no time, she was back at the palace, and presented the blackberries to her mother.

'Where did you get these?' spluttered the queen, who could not believe her eyes.

'In the forest,' said Anna, for something at the back of her mind told her not to mention the twelve little helpers by the fire.

'Well, you'd better get off to bed, and don't disturb your sister, Jezebella. She's been trying to get to sleep like a good girl while you've been roaming about at all hours.'

Annie said nothing but went gratefully off to bed and fell into a deep dreamless sleep. Unless everything that had happened to her that night was a dream …

Christmas passed with little merriment and no word of the absent king. The queen was consumed by jealousy and determined to be rid of Annie. Jezebella could not care less as she was experimenting with her new toys, Instagram and Snapchat.

At the very end of December, the queen instructed Annie to go into the forest and gather the first snowdrops. 'Your sister Jezebella and I are so sad that the king has not come home. We must be cheered up with some fresh flowers.'

'But snow is still falling,' said Annie. 'I'm not sure there are any snowdrops yet. Not a single one has peeked through, even in the garden.'

'Of course there are snowdrops, out in the forest,' insisted the queen. 'Have you no feeling for your own mother? Here is a basket to fill with the flowers. And don't think of coming back until you have it full.'

So, Annie wrapped up warmly once more and headed into the forest with the empty basket on her arm.

'That's the last we'll see of her,' thought the queen, gloating that this time the elder princess would not escape a well-deserved end.

As Annie walked through the forest, the snow seemed to get deeper and deeper. You could not see the ground where snowdrops might come through, as even beneath the trees everything was buried below mounds of white snow. Also, a fierce north wind was blowing through the bare branches, driving the falling flakes into her face. Darkness descended on the forest. The girl trudged on, but she was tiring and was about to give up and turn back when she saw that same glimmer of light ahead. Annie's heart rose and her step quickened.

As she drew towards the light it became stronger, and suddenly Annie was looking into that clearing amidst the trees. At its centre was a roaring log fire and round the fire sat the circle of little people huddled in rugs and shawls. Annie was delighted by that friendly sight.

'Come away in, lass, and welcome!' said the little king, with his long straggly beard and red woolly bonnet. 'Come and warm yourself up beside our fire.'

She went forward gladly. The wee men and women made room for her and soon she was sipping a hot fruity drink from a wooden beaker.

'Well,' said December, the Christmas king, 'what are you doing out again in the forest on a day like this?' Twelve pairs of little twinkling eyes settled on Annie.

'My mother, the queen, sent me out to look for snowdrops to cheer her and my sister up,' she explained.

'Well, well, your mother, you say. Very queenly she must be. It's not the time yet for snowdrops,' replied the little king kindly.

'I know. I can't find any in the garden or the forest.'

'Maybe we can help,' said the king, looking round the circle. 'January, would you be so good?' He gestured towards an old man with a white face and long, tangled white beard. As Annie looked, she realised his beard was full of icicles.

'Of course,' January said and gestured for the basket.

Someone beside Annie took the basket from her hands and passed it round the circle towards January, who then passed it on round. By the time it came back the basket was full to overflowing with snowdrops. Annie could not believe her eyes.

'There, there,' said the wee king, 'are you warmer now? You'd best be off home as this night is not going to improve on the day.'

'Thank you,' gasped Annie. 'I don't know how to thank you.'

'No need,' said January, in a low rasping voice. 'When you're frosty like me for centuries on end, winter flowers come naturally.'

'Bye bye,' chuckled the little king. 'We do enjoy your visits but it might be better not to come again soon.'

So off Annie went with a swift, sure step, feeling the wind behind her, while even the snow seemed less deep. In no time, she was back at the palace and presented the snowdrops to her mother.

'Where did you get these?' screeched the queen, grinding her teeth in disbelief.

'In the forest,' said Annie, for something at the back of her mind again warned her not to mention the twelve little helpers by the fire.

'Well, you'd better get off to bed, and don't disturb you sister, Jezebella. She's been trying to behave like a good, well-brought-up princess while you've been gadding about in the forest.'

Annie said nothing but went gratefully off to bed and fell into a deep dreamless sleep. Unless everything that had happened to her that day too had been a dream …

But the queen, her mother, could get neither rest nor sleep. She was consumed by hatred, and desperate to rid herself of Annie before the king, her father, returned. What could she send the wretched girl to do that would be truly impossible and ensure she never came back? She tossed and turned all night.

'Dearest Annie,' she hissed the next morning, 'I have word that our beloved king will be back in the next few days. You have done so well bringing blackberries and snowdrops, but what your father really desires and needs, and will have, is fresh strawberries.'

'Strawberries!' repeated Annie in disbelief.

'Yes, for I have heard that on the far side of the forest there is a rare crop of winter strawberries. Anyone who tastes that fruit will enjoy long life and freedom from pain. So, take this basket and bring it back full.' And she wanted to add, 'or don't come back at all' but she clenched her teeth to stop the words coming out and smiled thinly at Annie without opening her mouth.

So, Annie wrapped up warmly once more and headed into the forest with the empty basket on her arm. 'That's the last we'll see of her,' thought the queen. 'Finally. Strawberries are impossible in January, the silly little besom.'

As Annie walked through the forest, the snow seemed to have settled in deep, frozen drifts. You could not see the ground where anything might grow, far less strawberries. Also, a fierce north wind was blowing through the bare branches, driving frozen flakes like shards of ice into her face. Darkness descended on the forest. The girl trudged on, but she was tiring and was about to give up and turn back when she saw that same glimmer of light ahead. Annie's heart rose and her step quickened.

As she drew towards the light it became stronger, and suddenly Annie was looking into that clearing amidst the trees. At its centre was a roaring log fire and round the fire sat the circle of little people huddled in rugs and shawls. The girl was so relieved to see them.

'Come away in, lass, and welcome!' said the little king, with his long straggly beard and red woolly bonnet. 'Come and warm yourself up beside our little fire.'

She went forward gladly. The wee men and women made room for her and soon she was sipping a hot fruity drink from a wooden beaker.

'Well,' said the Christmas king, 'what are you doing out again in the forest on a day like this?' Twelve pairs of little twinkling eyes settled on Annie.

'My mother, the queen sent me out to look for strawberries for my father to eat when he comes home,' she explained doubtfully.

'Well, well, very queenly she must be, but a strange sort of mother. It's not the time for strawberries,' replied the little king.

'I know. I can't find any in the garden or the forest.'

'Maybe we can help,' said the king, looking round the circle. 'July, would you be so kind?' He gestured towards a little woman with golden hair and bright blue eyes winking out from her nut-brown face.

'Of course,' she said and gestured for the basket. Someone beside Annie took the basket from her hands and passed it round the circle towards July, who then passed it on round. By the time it came back the basket was full to overflowing with fragrant summer strawberries. Anna could not believe her eyes.

'There, there,' said the wee king, 'are you warmer now? You'd best be off home as this night is not going to improve on the day.'

'Thank you,' gasped Anna. 'I don't know how to thank you.'

'No need,' said July, in a mellow singsong voice. 'When you're sunny like me, from the top of your head to the tips of your toes, strawberries grow out of your fingers.'

'Bye bye,' said the Christmas king. 'We do enjoy your visits but I feel this might be your last for a while. Take care and good luck.'

So off Annie went with a swift, sure step, feeling the wind behind her, while even the snow seemed less deep. In no time, she was back at the palace, where she presented the full basket of strawberries to her mother.

The queen was speechless, incredulous and choking with fury. 'Where did you get these?' she gasped like a beached whale.

'In the forest,' said Annie, and this time she told her mother the truth, right out. 'I met these little people around a fire in their clearing.'

'Little people? In a clearing?'

'Twelve of them.'

'Right, that's it. Jezebella! Get out of bed this instant. If these little elves can make strawberries in January, then they can make gold and jewels. This instant, you lazy, pampered little besom. We're going to the forest to get their treasure. As for you, Annie, we've heard quite enough.'

'But its freezing outside, and dark.'

'You'd better get off to bed, and I'll sort you out when we return. From now on, you can pay for your keep by working in the kitchen. There's no time to lose. Quickly, Jezebella. If she can do it, so can you.'

The queen headed off into the forest, dragging her complaining daughter behind her. They stumbled in the darkness, but the queen drove on as if possessed. At last, she had got the better of her older daughter.

The snow had settled in deep frozen drifts. You could not see the ground and a fierce north wind was blowing through the bare branches, driving frozen flakes like shards of ice into their faces. At last, soaked through and half-dead from cold, they found the clearing. It was empty and silent. In the centre were dead ashes from a fire inside a circle of blackened stones.

'Where are they? Come here now!' yelled the queen.

Her voice echoed into the forest and then died. Her daughter clung to her in sudden fear. The queen looked round. Which way had they come? Which way should they go? As she staggered off into the forest the wind redoubled, and the snow began to drift and to blanket the forest floor. Once you lay down, unable to walk any further, the snow would cover you over for the rest of the winter.

When the king eventually returned home it was as a widower. He grieved for his foolish wife and daughter, but Annie looked after the palace and everyone in it with wisdom and kindness beyond her years. And in each season of the year, working in the garden and wandering in the forest, she thought of Earth's twelve helpers, and the different gifts they brought every month. But she always had a special place in her heart for blackberries, snowdrops and ripe summer strawberries.

Bringing in the Year

Long ago, men and women, boys and girls, animals and birds, lived through winter, spring, summer, autumn and winter again, much as we do, despite some climate changes. But it was different because, apart from winter ice, there were no fridges or freezers. So, our ancestors, even within living memory, had to dry, smoke, pickle and store, so they could get through the lean months when very little grew.

At the start of a new year, they looked forward to the season changing and the sun's return. This was a moment to celebrate and to share some of their precious stores of food. Life would once again prove bigger than any one person's needs, wants or desires. It was time to rest and party, even if things had been tough.

When was this new year? It might begin with the midwinter solstice, with Yule that became Christmas, Twelfth Night, Hogmanay in Scotland, New Year's Day, or even well into January with 'Old New Year', as people stubbornly hung on to the twelve days 'taken from them' by the Gregorian Calendar.

Whatever the celebration was called, it involved visiting and hospitality, with food and drink from the winter stores. There were customs and traditions surrounding such visits; these were named first-footing, wassailing, guising or mumming, in different places. There were rhymes and songs calling on people to open up their doors:

> O man, rise up and be not sweir [reluctant]
> Prepare against the Gude New Year,
> My New Year gift thou has in store,
> Gif me thy hart I ask no more.

Wassailers might sing:

> A wassail, a wassail, throughout all the town,
> Our cup it is white and our ale it is brown,
> Our wassail is made of the good ale and true,
> Some nutmeg and ginger, the best we could brew.

In all cases, the visitors would insist that they were not beggars but 'neighbours you have seen before'. Some would go on to sing in return for their supper, while others presented a mummers' play with a hero, a villain, conflict, death and resurrection. Contributions of food and drink still applied though as the last act:

> Blessed be the master o' tis house, and the mistress too
> And all the little bairnies that round the table grew.
> Their pockets full of money, the bottles full of beer –
> A Merry Christmas, Guisers, and a Happy New Year!

For gardeners, wassailing brought an extra benefit, when the guisers proceeded into the orchard and toasted the trees, often with cider in a wassailing bowl or bucket!

Old Apple Tree we wassail thee and hope that thou will bear,
For Lord doth know where we will be till apples come another year;
To bloom well and to bear well, so merry let us be,
Let every man take off his hat and shout out to thee, old Apple Tree.
Old Apple Tree, we wassail thee, and hope that thou will bear,
Hat fulls, cap fulls, three bucket bag fulls,
And a little heap under the stair.

Who could ask for more? Or for a more auspicious start to another growing season? With the upsurge of community gardens and orchards, these customs have found a fresh lease of life.

Ranting Roving Robin

It was late January in Scotland, when a wild storm blew in from the Atlantic Ocean onto the Ayrshire coast. With the storm came gale-force winds, hail, sleet and snow, blasting the towns and little villages across the south-west.

Among the victims was a recently built cottage in Alloway, which was surrounded by a market garden. The young gardener, William Burns, had worked hard with his own hands to build the cottage, as well as establish his gardening business on the outskirts of the prosperous county town of Ayr. His heavily pregnant wife Agnes was about to give birth to their first child.

As the storm's fury mounted, the labour began, and William had to set out to fetch a midwife. But the River Doon was in full flood. He had to wade across and the carry the stranded midwife over on his back through the raging waters. William was a determined man and his son Robert, who was born that night, was always to admire and respect his father, even when pursuing a completely different path through life.

The baby boy was safely delivered. But in the course of that tempestuous night, his first on Earth, the gable end of William's gardener's cottage gave way and collapsed. The young family was given shelter in a neighbour's house until the storm had subsided and the cottage could be rebuilt.

Some days after the birth, when the storm had receded, an old wise woman called in to see Agnes and her new baby. Some say she was a tinker, a woman of the Travelling People, who are reputed to have the second sight. She looked at the squalling little scrap of life in the cradle that William had made. Then the old woman took the baby's perfect, tiny, soft hand in her dirty, calloused fingers, and she peered at Robert's palm – his 'loof'.

'Ah,' says she, 'this waly boy will be nae coof [fool]. He'll hae misfortunes great an sma, but aye a hert abune them aa.'

That, at least, was how family tradition remembered the words. Maybe the old biddy was just keen to please, or perhaps the wise woman saw in this baby boy the full-grown poet of love and social justice that Robert Burns was to become. The same poet recalled these events in a rollicking song about Robin the 'ranter', or poet:

There was a lad was born in Kyle,
But whatna day or whatna style,
I doubt it's hardly worth the while
To be sae nice wi Robin.

Robin was a rovin boy,
Rantin, rovin, rantin, rovin,
Robin was a rovin boy,
Rantin, rovin, Robin!

But Robert's recollections of his birth and upbringing went deeper. He was always aware of the harsh changes faced by humans and animals alike in surviving and carving out a living. He became a passionate advocate of fellow feeling – for the harvest mouse, whose nest his plough had upturned, and even for the daisy trodden casually underfoot.

In later life, Robert followed the old New Year tradition of feeding the animals first in the morning. We know about his dog, Luath, the pet sheep, Mallie, and his faithful mare, Meg, who was to have a starring role rescuing the errant hero in Burns' famous tale of 'Tam O Shanter'.

It is surely no accident that Robert Burns' most celebrated poem, sung across the world at New Year and on his 25 January birthday, is a hymn to kindness. The imagined setting is of old friends gathered at a fireside in a cottage, like the one at Alloway in which the poet had come into the world in such dramatic circumstances:

Should auld acquaintance be forgot
And never brocht tae mind
Should auld acquaintance be forgot
And auld langsyne?

For auld langsyne, my jo,
For auld langsyne;
We'll tak a cup o kindness yet
For auld langsyne.

FEBRUARY

Snowdrops have bridged January and February. Their clumps of nodding white heads seem more reassuring than the false dawn of some flowering trees. The general colour scheme remains wanly green or grey, neither alive nor dead. My struggle with knotted ivy continues, a war of attrition with little apparent progress. The weather remains benign, reminding us that 'if Candlemas be fine and clear, there'll be two winters in that year'.

Then, with shocking suddenness, huge storms blow in from the Atlantic dispelling any seasonal languor. According to the forecasters, the Arctic vortex, not so far north of Edinburgh, has retained its frozen-plated integrity this winter. Normally it breaks down every so often, allowing cold air to flood Britain and Ireland, as briefly in December. But now it is keeping its Arctic fastness frozen, which is good news for polar bears, while leaving us exposed to the full force of the jet stream.

As wind and lashing remain are unleashed, normal garden activity is suspended. Where do all the birds go? While humans cower indoors, they must hunker down in scrub and shrub to await calmer air. Any temptation on the part of hibernating hedgehogs, butterflies or newts to stir is repressed. Life goes undercover.

Of course, the Celtic storytellers had their own explanation for all this. The mother goddess or creator – the Cailleach – is enraged by any early signs of spring. She calls up the wild creatures of storm, hail and flood to reimpose her harsh grip on the land. Her winter reign has not yet ended. Yet, despite the wisdom of these old warnings, we appear surprised by this latest twist in our meteorological fortunes.

Suddenly, the wind and water are the whole tale. Those early blossoms are blasted, though the snowdrops seem unperturbed. The burns turn into rivers and spill over the parklands. At one time, these winter floods were allowed to cover the still-agricultural lower flats to disperse sewage from the town and fertilise the soil for grazing or cropping. Now that the land has been developed, elaborate flood defences have been created to culvert and hem in the waters. They rush seawards, carrying with them the litter and detritus of our disposable culture to pollute our blue planet.

In nature, every action brings its own consequences. Will we only learn that lesson when it is too late? Are we so smart that we will come up with some means of keeping narrowly ahead? Not according to stories handed down by the ancestors. Our tricks have a persistent habit of redounding on our own heads.

For two weeks the batterings and soakings continue without remission. Fortunately, the trees are bare and less likely to suffer damage. Herons, ducks, geese and swans shelter as they can on the edges of the lochs as water levels rise. Every so often, a hungry fox patrols the gardens, stalking along the top of the estate wall and jumping down to investigate any promising sign of food.

Till, overnight, cold air moves in and brings snow. This seems like an unexpected novelty, so I take my grandchildren up to the hills where they race about like demented escapees from cabin fever. There is a frozen crust on the first fall that gives way with a satisfying crunch, but unfortunately on the slower slopes this conceals slush, and they stretch their lengths like human sledges. Time for some of that winter vegetable broth at last.

Between bouts of snow, frost resumes a grip, and there are some crystal-sharp mornings, and dramatic night skies as if moon, stars and planets need to shine, each with their distinctive lustre.

One morning, in late February, flag iris appears in the narrow, sheltered border by our front door. They are intensely blue, with a tongue of gold inside the petals. Fragile, yet breathtakingly hardy, they have absorbed energy and heat in this sunny, summer spot. Now they give back the glory of that season in intense bursts. Despite flood and now frost, they are harbingers of the daffodils and crocuses that will soon follow.

We have birthed a new season, winter-spring. Is this the shape of things to come?

First and Last

The most important thing we look forward to in springtime are the colours that come back into a winter world of grey and brown. Yet, this was not always so. In fact, at one time there were no colours in the world at all.

The Creator had been so busy making shapes and sizes of all kinds that that she had forgotten about colours. But one day, the birds came to visit her and complain.

'Look,' they said, 'no one can tell us apart. We are the same dull drab grey. It's boring, and it's not safe as we keep crashing into each other when we fly.'

The Creator could see immediately that this was a problem, and not at all in line with her plan to create a beautiful universe.

So, she asked one of her angels to bring a paintbox and she began immediately to mix an immaculate range of colours in every hue. Imagine how many shades there were!

The birds were delighted and pushed forward to get as much colour as they could. The peacock got a bit of nearly every red, green and blue in the box. The hummingbird swooped down just in time to collect some green and blue. The parrot squawked for his share, getting scarlet, green and orange. The flamingo settled for a spread of pinks.

And so it went on all day, with birds fluttering down and the Creator painting every one, until often she was just touching a wingtip or tail with her brush. Eventually, she was done, and began to pack away her brushes, when a little cheep sounded on her shoulder. There was a tiny grey bird there, looking very sad.

'You've forgotten me,' he said.

'Oh dear,' said the Creator. 'I am so sorry, but I've run out of paints for today.'

'Wait, just a moment,' said the wise snowy owl. 'These other birds have lots of colours. If they all give one little speck each then this little bird will not be left out.'

And that is what happened. They all gave one little speck of red and green and golden yellow, until the little grey bird had the most beautiful, brightly coloured feathers of all the birds. And he was called the goldfinch.

Away all the birds flew in their bright new coats. And all the flowers looked up at this multi-coloured display. Then of course they wanted colours too. So, the next day the angel brought new paints and the Creator went round happily painting all the flowers. That is why we have red poppies and blue violets, and yellow daffodils and pink tulips, and blossoms in all the colours of the rainbow.

It was a long, busy day but finally every flower had a colour and the paint box was empty once more. Then, suddenly, hidden

away in the woods, the Creator spotted a tiny flower with perfect, tightly formed petals nodding towards the ground.

'Oh, little flower,' she said, 'I am so sorry, but I will have to make you pure white. I have no colours left.'

The little flower seemed to droop lower. Then the Creator had a flash of inspiration.

'But you will be the first,' she said. 'The very first flower to appear as winter ends. And your white petals will shine out and give everyone hope that spring is coming, even if there is still snow covering the ground. You will be called Snowdrop.'

The little flower waved its head with joy. And ever since then, Snowdrop has been the first flower of the year, and the sign of Bride, the gentle goddess of spring.

Town Mouse and Country Mouse

Once there was a mouse family who lived very comfortably in an old stone house. At the front it faced onto a street with shops and behind there was a long garden with fruit, flowers and vegetables. The mice lived in a dry, cosy space beneath the floorboards and were able to gather food in the garden by day and come out at night to forage for tasty titbits left around the house.

Now mother mouse had a cousin who was a field mouse and lived with her family out in the country. When summer came, the town mice were invited to go and stay. The little mice from the town had never had so much space in which to play, and they ran through the fields digging endless tunnels and playing hide and seek with their little cousins.

The weather was lovely and country mouse had built her nest safely on the field verge where they were not bothered by the farmer. There was lots of grain to eat, along with some dried beans that the country mouse had stored. But that was all.

'Do you always eat the same food?' asked town mouse, despondently.

'Not at all,' said her country cousin. 'We have different things to eat each season according to the crops. So soon there will be lots of potatoes and barley, and then turnips in wintertime.'

'Well,' commented town mouse, 'I am sure it is all very wholesome, but a bit dull, you must admit. You should come to visit us in the winter and sample some of our shop delicacies.'

'Very well,' responded country mouse amiably, 'that will be nice for the little ones to see town life.'

'Country bumpkins,' squeaked town mouse, beneath her whiskers. And, truth be told, she was relieved to get back to her own house and a diet of cheese, bread, cake, fruit and munchy green vegetables from her garden.

However, as promised, country mouse and her children came to stay in the town, after Christmas when the weather was very cold and food in the country quite hard to find. The country cousins settled in quickly to an extension beneath the floorboards and were soon chasing the townie children round the garden and playing hide and seek.

Country mouse was amazed at all the stores of food in the house, not least the cheeses and smoked hams. Then there was bread and fruit loaf aplenty and still some winter vegetables in the garden. At night, town mouse took her cousin round the kitchen, where all kind of succulent sweet morsels lay beneath the tables and inside the cupboards. The country folk had never fed so well and were slowing down with weight.

One evening, the two mother mice were sitting contentedly cleaning their whiskers when all the children burst squealing into their house. The country cousins were shaking in terror.

'The cat sneaked up on us,' explained the townie mice, 'but we ran for it!'

'It was a monster,' quaked the country mice, 'with claws like razors and supersonic speed. We don't want to go out there ever again.'

'There, there,' soothed country mouse. 'I am sure you will learn to watch out for this cat.'

'Maybe it could be fitted with a bell,' smiled town mouse, 'to warn the children when it's coming.'

'Who would put a bell on the cat?' asked country mouse nervously.

That night, the two mother mice went out to stock up with dainties. Country mouse had just slipped under the pantry door when she heard town mouse squeak, 'watch out it's the cat!', as her cousin fled beneath the floorboards through a mousehole.

The cat realised the mice were about and scratched at the pantry door. As she peered out in terror, country mouse could see the claws by the light of the moon, and the cat's mouth drawn back over its ferocious teeth. She was trapped in the pantry for more than two hours, until the cat lost interest and went off after other prey.

When country mouse eventually reached the others under the floorboards, she was still in shock and could not stop trembling. 'It was terrible,' she shuddered. 'Never again!'

'We told you, Mum,' said her children, 'but you didn't believe us.'

The next morning, country mouse packed up to return home. 'Thank you for having us,' she told her cousin, 'but I think we must go home.'

'Why? You're wasting your time out in that wilderness,' scolded town mouse. 'After all, a mouse only lives for so long and you have to enjoy things while you can.'

'Well, cousin, I would rather eat my barley grains in peace than have all your luxuries and live in fear.'

And off country mouse went with her children in tow and, good as her word, she never visited her town cousin again.

Rat and Weasel

Many birds and animals go hungry in February as winter ends, but not the Weasel, or 'Whittret', as he is called in Scotland. A tiny flash of teeth and muscle, weighing no more than four ounces, Weasel is a fierce hunter and fighter, and sometimes in the heat of battle he kills for the sake of killing.

Weasel eats mice, voles, baby rabbits and small birds he catches on the ground. But his greatest enemy is Rat. That is why Weasel loves to raid farmyards. But in the town, our extended community garden, surrounded by ditches and rough ground, is his ideal hunting ground.

Once, long ago, when this land was still a wealthy estate, the gardener lived in a cottage adjacent to his lord's walled garden. You can still see its tumbledown walls. The little cottage had its own bit of land, where William, the gardener, could grow vegetables for his own family, and sit out to rest after a hard day's work. In fact, it was his habit in all seasons, when he got home after work, to draw some water from the pump into an old tin bath, take off his boots and wash his dirty feet before going inside. No one wore socks in those days!

One late February day, which had been unseasonably warm, he was enjoying the feel of the cold water around his weary feet when he heard a fierce squealing and screeching near the garden wall. Getting up to investigate, he saw a weasel and a rat locked in mortal combat.

The quarrel seemed to be about a shrew that Weasel had snatched but which Rat had decided was his property. The struggle was fierce as Weasel rushed in and seized Rat by the throat. But Rat was four times bigger and heavier than Weasel. He managed to tear Weasel off and pinned him to the ground with his fierce claws, closing in for the kill. Would Weasel wriggle and bite his way free or were his moments on earth now numbered?

Without thinking, William stepped forward and stamped on Rat's body, forgetting that his foot was bare. Immediately Weasel slipped free, bloodied but unbowed, and made his escape. But Rat turned ferociously and sunk his teeth into William's foot. As he cried in pain, Rat too fled the scene.

The gardener hobbled back and dipped his foot into the cold water. Then he went inside and thought no more of it. But that night his foot began to swell up, and by morning the poison was travelling up toward his knee, leaving his lower leg distended, black and blue.

William sat by the fire with his swollen leg stretched out on a stool. His wife tried every salve and poultice she knew, with no effect. In desperation, she decided to go into the village to consult a wise woman of her acquaintance. Her ailing husband was left dosing fitfully and feverishly by the fire.

At one point, William thought he saw a blur of movement by the door. He rubbed his eyes and little Weasel appeared by his leg with its mouth full of leaves. In a single agile scamper, the weasel was on the stool and laid the leaves gently on his wounded foot. Then, in the flash of an eye, Weasel was away. Only to return in a few minutes with more leaves!

Three times Weasel made this journey, or at least three times of which William was aware, for he sank into a deep slumber. By the time his wife returned from the wise woman, the swelling was subsiding. That night, William was able to rest in his bed, and by the next morning he could place his whole weight on the healing foot.

The first thing William did was to gather up the leaves and bury them at his garden wall, where the terrible battle had taken place. The storytellers who passed on this old tale do not name the plants or herbs involved. Perhaps it was dog's mercury? Whatever, from then on, William always allowed wild plants and herbs to flourish along his garden wall, and though his cottage is now a ruin, some of them are still there today.

MARCH

March brings light with lengthening days. One morning, a strengthening band of light lies along Craigmillar's wooded ridge on the horizon. Above that, exactly aligned, sits a thick mass of grey cloud, as if some abstract painter had drawn a watercolour brush across the canvas in one single firm stroke.

As the sun rises further above the horizon the cloud sinks. The two realms begin to merge. For a few moments the grey mass is translucent, transfused by light. But the cloud regains its strength, and the light is suppressed – for now at least. By rising early, I have witnessed an intense seasonal drama. A spectacle of nature played out over my urban dwelling place.

And in truth, the season is still uncertain which way to go. Storm and snow have receded, but the wind freshens with the day and showers chase rolling clouds across blue skies. The landscape seems latent, as in Thomas Hardy's 'A Backward Spring':

The trees are afraid to put forth buds,
and there is timidity in the grass;
The plots lie grey where gouged by spuds,
and whether next week will pass
Free of sly sour winds is the fret of each bush
of Barberry waiting to bloom.

Yet, everywhere are harbingers of new light – from the golden tongues of flag iris to the trumpets of daffodils.

The garden chores are also waiting on this uncertain outcome. Too soon to sow seeds, even in my little greenhouse that frosts so easily on a cold morning. Any lingering dieback can be cleared from the herbaceous border, but it is too soon to weed for fear of disturbing bulbs and early primroses. The epic ivy prune continues but it seems a never-ending task to disentangle the interlacing woody growth that should have been tackled three or four years ago. It is remarkable how, when denied any further upright support, ivy winds in around itself and keeps growing. As ivy flowers at this time of year, the leaves simplify their shape, and all the energy goes into future growth. But now I have pitted my own determined will against its green force. Gardening sometimes requires compromise.

I take an afternoon off to follow the stream across the parklands, past Arthur's Seat. The graceful silver birches are sheathed in purple as their buds swell. On elders and hazels, the catkins hang ripe to fall and seed. Tree sparrows, tits, finches and wrens are vocal, and I spot one fast-moving brown dipper, a pledge of cleaner waters, though, as yet, no kingfisher is to be seen. Rooks are now in earnest building up their twiggy piles in the tall treetops.

There are plentiful signs of burrowing voles and tunnelling moles. I wonder if the hedgehogs have woken up yet. Maybe they should stay under the duvet for a little longer, just in case.

Mid-month, as the spring equinox approaches, frost returns, interchanging with snow showers that lie white on distant hills. The ground is unfrozen beneath a surface crust, so I intersperse digging in the shrubbery with more ivy cutting. It beggars belief how root systems extend invisibly. Without some hard pushback, some shrubs would undermine the lawn and extend into the vegetable beds. Such are the perils of diversity in a smaller garden. Down in the earth, winter has long receded, if it ever had an icy grip below.

Inevitably, these activities lead to visits to the recycling centre in the former Craigmillar quarry. This is where medieval builders found the honey-warm sandstone that still features in Edinburgh's oldest buildings – John Knox House and Holyrood Palace. Now, a hardworking team of men and women lead the fight to protect our ecosystems from further damage.

Having tipped three big bags of ivy and roots into the garden waste, I come home by Craigmillar Castle with its unrivalled views of Arthur's Seat and the Firth of Forth. But right above me, a huge rainbow has formed, bridging the hill and Edmonstone Rise. It is so close that the colours are viscous, moist. The stems are thick and the arch dominant. Am I in the rainbow? Then suddenly I am through; it is on my right side, and before me are showers chasing over the cold blue sea. I stop to draw breath and wonder at what I saw; to ponder again at how nature transforms what we see moment to moment.

After a few more equinoctial days of sun and showers, including some sleet, March plays out its dramas with a cumulative push towards new beginnings. Days become warm and sunny, with nights cool, yet barely frosted. The worms rise en masse to the top of the compost bin to meet the sun. Bulbs are opening their paint boxes, and finally the gardener's New Year is beginning. There seems to be an indrawn breath of pure enjoyment, recalling Wordsworth's call to his sister:

It is the first mild day of March:
Each minute sweeter than before;
The redbreast sings from the tall larch
That stands beside our door.

There is a blessing in the air,
Which seems a sense of joy to yield
To the bare trees, and mountains bare,
And grass in the green field.

My sister! ('tis a wish of mine)
Now that our morning meal is done,
Make haste your morning task resign,
Come forth and feel the sun.

No joyless forms shall regulate
Our living calendar:
We from today, my friend, will date
The opening of the year.

Love, now a universal birth
From heart to heart is stealing.
From earth to man, from man to earth;
It is the hour of feeling.

Clever Crow, Wily Fox

As winter ends, while the garden is still bare, you become more aware of the active crows. Everyone knows that crows are the cleverest of birds, and that applies to their whole extended family. Ravens are bearers of wisdom and harbingers of doom. Rooks have been known to hold parliaments, standing in a solemn circle, and to conduct trials of offending members of their society. Jackdaws live in colonies and move from place to place together following an organised plan.

In Britain, jays and magpies are the most handsome crows. The jay is a multi-coloured dandy, while magpies only reveal their iridescent plumage on closer examination – green, purple and azure, with touches of crimson. They operate in pairs, or small groups formed from pairs, and are regular garden visitors. Magpies can be merciless and piratical towards other birds, yet they also exhibit fellow feeling. Magpies have been seen grieving round a fallen companion, crooning a lament and laying grass over the corpse.

But sociability does not stretch to the carrion crow, or its equivalent in northern Scotland, the hoodie craw. They are lone operators along with one mate. A famous folk song, 'The Twa Corbies', describes a carrion crow telling its mate about a 'fallen knight' lying behind a stone dyke. They agree to share out the best bits of flesh – an eye, and the marrow of a breastbone. No one else knows that the knight is dead meat, except for 'his hawk, his hound, and his lady fair', but they have all moved on to fresh pastures – hunting or a new mate. In a final macabre touch, the corbies agree to thatch their nest with the corpse's long blond hair, as the wind blows through his bleached bones.

One time, a solitary crow came into the garden at the beginning of March, scavenging for scraps through the lean times. Imagine his delight at finding a lump of orange cheese. Up he went into a big bare-branched elm tree above the garden wall. There he perched proudly, exhibiting his find for all to see. Time to enjoy his cleverness, before consuming the plunder.

It so happened that on this same day, a lean, wiry, russet-red fox came along the top of the garden wall. He was on the same scavenging quest as the crow. These last weeks had been among winter's hardest, even though the weather was a bit warmer. The orange cheese caught his sharp eye, which then fixed on the beak firmly clamped round this delicious morsel, and finally the beady stare above.

'Why, Mister Crow,' said the fox huskily, 'what an extraordinarily clever fellow you are. All the choicest titbits are at your command. No human, far less an animal or bird, can rival your skill and intelligence. You always make off with the winning prize.'

The crow preened his dark feathers and almost opened his beak to caw in throaty assent, but then thought better of it. A choked off 'craiai-k' was all that came out round the cheese.

'What was that, Mister Crow?' enquired the fox politely. 'You do have the most beautiful voice of all the birds, among your many other fine qualities.'

Then he hurried on before the crow might respond, or even fly off. 'It is, of course, true that many other birds are praised for their fine singing, here in the garden. The blackbird has a melodious trill, the thrush an outpouring of liquid song, and at night beyond the confines of any garden the nightingale regales the human ear. And of course, in spring on the hillside, the cuckoo … '

Up on his branch, the crow flapped his wings, impatient at this stream of praise for other lesser birds.

'But of course, Mister Crow, forgive me. You are so right. No feathered creature, or for that matter any furred or scaly one, can match your musical prowess. When you open your beak wide …'.

The crow's breast puffed out with pride.

'… you send forth an irrepressible torrent of song, it is like a …'

The crow's jaw twitched.

'… like a well-oiled machine gun – nay, an orchestra of melodious sounds swelling over this garden.'

The crow's beak opened, and he launched into a harsh croak of irrepressible pride and pleasure. And his lump of orange cheese fell straight into the fox's waiting mouth. Before the crow had paused to draw breath, Mister Fox had jumped down into the next garden and slipped away to enjoy his tasty snack in private.

Oh, vain crow, and wily flattering fox. In truth, you rival each other in the harsh vocal stakes. Why do we see our foolish and deceiving selves in you?

Tim Vole

That was all I heard – a little plop – as I sat quietly by the stream that runs along the side of the allotments. That is how to see a water vole – watch and listen.

Tim Vole had been feeding from new green grass on the bank, but something had made him dive back in and swim to the other side. Look, there are the tiny bubbles from his breath. Now we can see his head with its sharp black eyes and blunt nose and whiskers. Maybe he will clamber into his little hole in the river bank, and we will see his tail, which is only half the length of his body.

What a neat, clean little creature is Tim, quite different from the much larger brown river rats with which voles are often confused. Brown rats will eat anything in the allotments, and often do, but voles are vegetarians, and busy workers, like miniature beavers. They are inquisitive and shy, not garden pests.

In December Tim had collected leaves and green plants to line his burrow. Through the winter he gnawed on roots and tree bark, but now it is March, and the first green grass is growing, and the voles are out. They are not very sociable, guarding their little stretch of the bank with its burrows and galleries. Tim has his own wife, though, and five embryo voles are already growing inside her.

One day at the beginning of May, these quints are born – blind, helpless, pink scraps of life, feeding on their mother's milk. But deep in the bank in a prepared nest of leaves and dried grass, they are perfectly safe. Safe, that is, from the weasels, stoats, rats and hawks that will hunt them later on in their grown-up lives.

And that was spring. By early summer, the young voles are outside feeding for themselves. Their mother is already expecting more babies and has no time for unruly adolescents. Tim snaps at his offspring impatiently. Soon they will have to make their own way in the world. But for now, he keeps them in the territory that he marks out each night with his droppings.

There is lots of food now with grasses and river weed, and minnows in the stream or occasionally young frogs. But there are dangers for the young voles. A heron comes fishing. With big, lazy wing flaps, he comes up from the loch and along the stream till he finds a stance. There he waits and watches, still as a pole. A young vole scampers out and the heron's neck snakes forward at speed. The little vole is speared on his beak and down the long, grey throat it goes – a tasty warm morsel for the big bird. Now there are four young voles in Tim's river bank.

July turns into August's lazy heat. In the allotments, all the plants have grown tall, waving in a gentle breeze. There are potatoes, cauliflowers, cabbages and runner beans. The water in the stream is low and a bit smelly. The sharp-toothed water rats living downstream raid Tim's river bank and kill mother vole's new babies.

But the four young voles are safe. They are fast and agile, and they stay out playing and eating all hours. They are interested in mating too now, sniffing for female voles as dusk falls. And that is when the tawny owl swoops from the nearby trees. He drops fast, with wings outspread, and snatches up a young vole. Up and away she goes, crushing the life out of the terrified creature. In her nest, the voracious owlets will peck and tear and gobble. Now there are three young water voles. And that was summer.

In September the weather breaks with thunder, lightning and lashing rain. Burns and drains poured into the stream, and within three hours it is an ugly, rising swell of water, climbing the banks and flooding the burrows. But the young voles are fine. They retreat far into the bank where Tim and his ancestors have constructed a labyrinth of higher galleries. But mother vole was bunched up in a burrow with her third helpless litter of babies, and they all drowned.

Yet this tragedy barely touches the three fit survivors. Autumn is heaven, with sunny days and showers. There is an abundance of carrots, beans and apples in the plots. The young adults get clever, scampering in the shade of the plants, pulling down pods and making off with crunchy, juicy beans. The water is flowing clean now, and they plop, plonk and splash, stirring up the sediment as they swim in and out of the lower burrows.

But father Tim is getting old now and much slower. He cannot keep order by snapping and nipping. The young voles push him off and ignore him in the arrogance of their prime. Tim crawls into a deep burrow to die quietly, as he has mainly lived, alone. And that was autumn.

Winter comes in frosty with cutting east winds. The vegetables have been dug up, apart from leeks, winter parsnips and Brussels sprouts clenched to their stalks. The young adult voles cannot stay out of their burrows for long in case they freeze. In special chambers deep in the bank, they hoard green plants and grasses to see them warmly through the hard, iron days when they will have to gnaw at roots and bark.

The voles must not wander too far from the stream for the ground is hard and shelterless. Humans come to dig their winter vegetables from the frozen earth. And there is a fox living on the allotments, dug in under a little-visited shed, foraging daily on the compost heaps. At the far end of the site an old man leaves food out for the fox.

Two days after Christmas – a cold, dark, frozen day – the voles are thin and shivery. They must find more food in the short hours of light. So, they leave the bank and cut across the path towards a compost heap. Under the covers they go, scratching, pulling and nibbling – cabbage leaves, potato peelings, a piece of mouldy bread. They scramble out, weighed down with their plunder, and the fox pounces.

He has been sloping along the boundary fence, watching. Spotting the movement beneath the compost covers, he switches onto a diagonal, and closes in silently on his prey. Rapidly, he scoops the first two voles up into his mouth as they unwarily emerge. The third drops his rations and runs, making it back to the burrows. The last vole does not come out again for a long time. And that was winter.

It was March before the first young grasses pushed up again on the bank of the stream. A vole sniffed the warm air from the mouth of his burrow. With a plop he slipped into the water, chestnut brown, blunt-nosed and whiskered like a neat little beaver. Swimming strongly, he leaves his old stretch of the bank, a handsome dark-eyed water vole with a tail half the length of his body, looking for a mate. Father and mother they will become, beside the allotments. Now once more it is spring.

Fussy Wren

People say there are more wrens in Britain and Ireland than any other kind of bird. That seems incred- ible, because they are secretive little creatures who keep a low profile amidst hedges and bushes, so we do not see them as often as other birds. Sometimes they were called the 'bird-mouse' and scientists call them 'troglodytes', as if they lived in caves!

But wrens are little atoms of energy. They sing louder than most other birds, and with their short, stumpy wings, wrens whirr past at speed into another patch of undergrowth. They are great sur- vivors and in the coldest winters, wrens, who normally love their own company, pile into a sheltered space together to keep warm.

Yet what is little known about wrens is that they are fussy. Look at their beautifully built, domed nests – like a perfectly formed egg with a tiny hole for a door. The outside is formed from leaves and moss, while the inside is lined with feathers and even wool. However, the female wren is not content with this work of art. She needs at least six nests from which she can choose the best, after minutely inspecting every single one inside and out.

So, the male wren must construct all these nests, while also singing his heart out, whirring his wings to attract his mate and chasing off any rivals. Eventually, the female wren settles into her chosen abode and lays some eggs. You might think the male would now be exhausted. He certainly takes little interest in the hatching eggs. Instead, he builds another six nests and tries to entice a second female. Perhaps he is fussy too, or just a bit false-hearted. At any rate, there are plenty of chicks to keep the wren tribe going.

Maybe, though, the wrens are choosy because they remember that they are actually king and queen of all the birds? This happened long ago, when the birds had no ruler, so they came together one day to decide who should be their king.

What a bustle and stir and raucous screeching there was, as seagulls and ravens, hawks and herons, larks and sparrows, hoopoes and cuckoos all insisted they should reign as kings and queens. Peacock said the most beautiful bird should be chosen, gannet said the one which could dive deepest, nightingale said the sweetest singer, and so forth.

Finally, the wise old owl suggested that whichever bird could fly nearest the sun should be crowned. They all agreed and were soon practising their best swoops and soars. As it turned out, there was not much of a competition, since eagle could outclimb every other bird. Up and up, he went, now gliding and then soaring sunwards. Clearly he would be king.

Yet, as eagle neared the sun it became hotter and hotter. He felt he had gone high enough and levelled off. 'Now I can be king,' he thought proudly. But just as he hovered ready to swoop down, a tiny little bird that had hidden in eagle's feathers, fluttered up another few inches and then dropped back onto the great bird's broad back. In the process, the wren, for it was a wren, singed his tail feathers, leaving him just a short sticking-up tail. He did not care a bit, singing out loudly, 'I'm the king of the birds! I flew the highest!'

And all the birds assembled below had to agree.

But they did not want this brown tiddler with a short tail to be their king. Instead, they arrested the wren for cheating and trickery. The brave little wren was imprisoned in a mousehole and the owl was put on guard duty. Then the other birds went off to rest and feed.

The little wren was terrified. What would they do to him the next day? As darkness fell, he tried to sneak out, but the owl kept one eye open and pecked at him. But after a time, the owl got sleepy and closed his other eye. Like a flash, the wren was out and away.

That is why, ever since, most wrens stay hidden in low-lying bushes, hedges and ditches. One exception, though, is that a few wrens nest high up near an eagle's lair where they claim protection from hunters. As for the owl, he cannot be seen at all by day as all the other birds scold him for letting wee rascal wren escape his punishment. Yet, despite that, wrens are still true kings and queens; they have never forgotten their right to be choosy.

APRIL

We sense a surge of April waiting to break through and over us. But at first it comes in staged bursts of life and colour. The first responders are non-native though long-domiciled plants, which blazon their heraldic colours against a still restrained backcloth. White and pink magnolias unfurl to spectacular effect. The cherry blossoms are smaller, yet cluster abundant on the branches. Hibiscuses are ornate with crimson would-be roses. Darwin's barberry is covered with intense orange-red flowers and the Japanese quince is hung with exquisite bell blooms that will later transform into ornamental fruit.

These plants are the spring pride of suburban gardens. But in the wooded shelter belts, the native trees are reluctant to leaf too soon. Catkins and pussy willows, yes, but foliage, no. Because there is no shading canopy, the woodland floor produces a flowering carpet – once described as the cloak of Bride, goddess of spring. Wild garlic, the bear plant, is profuse and odorous. Rarer, yet precious, are the gentle subtle yellows of wild primrose. It is too early for bluebells but in sunnier spots celandines are opening.

In both garden and nearby woodland, birds are singing, marking out their mating territories and building nests. Sadly, the virtuoso outpourings of the song thrush have been missing in recent times, but blackbirds trill melodiously and the finches, sparrows, tits and chaffinches all emit their distinctive high-energy cheeps or tweets – no social media required. It is remarkable how few trees or bushes it takes to attract bird life. As average temperatures slowly rise, insects multiply to provide the birds with their essential food supplies.

In a different dynamic, magpies are skirmishing in airborne hostilities over nesting sites with rooks and jackdaws. I have dark suspicions that those streamlined, piratical magpies are also staking out the nests that they might rob over the next few weeks. They are among nature's handsomest aviators with their black-turquoise plumage, but they are serial predators, rapacious and totally ruthless, downing smaller birds, smashing shells and consuming nestlings of all species.

Bumblebees are especially eye-catching just now when vegetation is still sparse. They have been on the move since early March and fly around like airships in search of a dock. These big bees are all young queens who, having woken from hibernation, spend a few weeks feeding on pollen and soaking up whatever sunshine spring offers. Then, each chooses a nesting site in the undercover of a shrubbery or inside a field mouse or vole's former abode. Inside, she forms a circular chamber lined like a nest and in its centre a wax cup from her own secretions in which she lays her eggs and stores pollen. Next, she seals the cup into an enclosed cell, and makes a wax honeypot from which her grubs will feed when hatched. They will pupate in silk cocoons and then emerge as this summer's worker bees.

It took a long time for naturalists to sort out the hibernation–migration conundrum. It was into the twentieth century before it was firmly established that swallows, swifts and martins migrate in the winter to Africa. It seems counter-intuitive that such small birds should be capable of such long-distance flights. Equally, it seems unlikely that insects like bees can survive hibernation. Their life cycle is highly evolved to maximise the summer warmth.

Hibernation or migration also explains why in April we might see a small tortoiseshell, peacock or brimstone butterfly in the garden. They all hibernate. But some of the more glamorous species like red admirals and painted ladies migrate from southern Europe or north Africa, so we will not see them for a while to come.

Alas, spring sign spotting is not an activity that a working gardener can overindulge. Especially as April is proving dry and relatively warm compared to a steely March. We can no longer be held back. Completing the much-delayed vegetable bed dig is now urgent. The first seed potatoes can go in, albeit happed up with earth. Broad beans are also planted outside.

The main vegetable crops can be sown in seed trays in the greenhouse: lettuce, carrot, beetroot, cabbage, leeks, shallots, along with climbing beans, parsley, coriander, fennel and other herbs. Finding space for all this in my tiny greenhouse involves an intricate system of temporary shelves and the kind of patience required when packing a car for an outdoor holiday. But afterwards, there is satisfaction in a job well done.

The greenhouse was accommodated in this garden by excavating into the upper level of the sloping ground. So, on the side shaded by the house, it is partially below ground. This was in line with a wider design to give the garden more structure by converting the slope into three levels or terraces. The top level is shady and surrounded by an ivy hedge, which was not part of the ivy cull. There is a rockery there and within it a recessed bed of river pebbles amidst which I placed a statue of Janus, the two-faced god of time, who looks simultaneously forward and back.

The middle level, into which the greenhouse is set, contains the vegetable beds and fruit bushes. The third and lowest level has a small lawn with the herbaceous border on one side and the shrubbery on the other. At the very end are some small trees, including fruit trees, the old boundary wall, and the old brick patio. It surrounds a large sundial, dated 1843, which the first owner of this house erected in memory of a historic year in Scotland's religious and social history – the Great Disruption, or revolt against the Established Church and the Westminster laws that constrained it. More about Janus later.

For now, time is all forwards, and I must keep up. Having set the vegetables in motion, I need to weed the herbaceous border and loosen up the soil with a trowel. Working on hands and knees, I rehearse like an incantation my border design with its promise of summer: hostas, penstemons, hollyhocks, sea holly, globe thistles, lupins, delphiniums, helianthus, with some carnations at the front and Stachys Byzantinas, Gertrude Jekyll's favourite grey-green cover, to set off the colours. But will winter's depredations have left gaps? And how will they be filled?

Cherry Blossom

Though wild cherry trees grow in southern Britain, it is the flowering cherry tree that has come to brighten spring in gardens across the country. Beautiful flowering cherry trees come from Japan; their blossoms are abundant, delicate and short-lived.

Once, in a village in Japan, there was a grove of old cherry trees that grew beside the well in the centre of the houses. No one could remember a time when the cherry trees had not been there, and the villagers believed that a goddess dwelt in the grove and looked after their fortunes. Each year they eagerly awaited the arrival of the cherry blossom as a sign that their year would once again be blessed with plenty.

But one spring, a messenger arrived with a proclamation from the Emperor. He was going through all the villages announcing that a new temple was to be established in the capital city and every village must contribute material for its building. The messenger finished reading the scroll and then looked at the old cherry trees. 'Cherry is a good hard wood for carving,' he said. 'The Emperor's wagon will come soon to fetch your contribution.'

After the herald had left, the villagers broke out in complaint and lamentation. 'We cannot cut down our precious cherry trees!' they cried. 'For the goddess will abandon us for ever.'

But one young man, called Yasunari, remained calm. 'Listen,' he said, 'we don't have to cut down the cherry trees. I will organise a work party, with three carts drawn by our best oxen. We will go up into the mountain and cut some trees there for the Emperor's temple.'

And so it was. The village agreed to work together to follow Yasunari's plan. They went to the mountain and under the young man's instruction, they cut down two pine trees, a hardwood maple and a mountain ash. When the Emperor's waggoners arrived they loaded up the wood without question and departed for the capital with a full load.

Not long after these events, Yasunari came back to the village from working in the rice fields. He stopped by the well to take a drink of water, and as he lowered his jug, he noticed a young woman resting under the cherry trees.

'Good day,' he said. 'Are you a stranger here?'

'Yes,' she said, shyly. 'I was on a long journey to the capital city but felt very tired. When I saw these beautiful trees, I sat down in the shade to rest.'

'You are most welcome to our village,' said Yasunari politely. 'Will you come to my mother's house to share some food?'

'Thank you for your kindness,' the young woman said. Then she stood, bowed and followed Yasunari to his house, where she was hospitably received and refreshed with rice and vegetables. Soon, Yasunari's mother and the young woman were chatting happily and it was agreed that the traveller, who was called Cherry Blossom, should stay to recover her strength before resuming the journey.

Well, the day stretched into another week, and Yasunari and Cherry Blossom spent more and more time in each other's company. Soon, it was understood that they would marry, so that Cherry Blossom could become part of the family and live on in the village. Weeks became months, and another year, and Cherry Blossom gave birth to a lovely baby boy, who quickly became the apple of his grandmother's eye.

Meantime, rumours arrived from the capital city that work on the Emperor's great new temple was almost complete. But the villagers thought little of the Emperor's doings or his temple. Till one day, unexpectedly, the Emperor's herald appeared once again in the marketplace. The people gathered nervously to listen to his message.

'The Emperor's great temple is almost complete,' he announced, 'but, for the final carvings, more hard wood is immediately required. The Emperor is pleased to accept these cherry trees as an offering from your village.'

The villagers were aghast.

'No!' cried Cherry Blossom, 'not my trees!' and she ran home weeping.

But there was no time to object, or offer any other trees, because that very same day the Emperor's wagons and his wood-cutters arrived. They chopped down every one of the trees in the ancient cherry grove.

Yasunari watched sadly as the last wagon rolled out of the village. Then he turned for home. There, his little baby son was sleeping in his grandmother's arms, but there was no sign of Cherry Blossom.

'Where is my wife?' asked Yasunari.

'She was very upset,' replied his mother. 'She took a mantle and rushed out. I thought she was going to the grove.'

'No, she wasn't there when they cut the trees,' said Yasunari, going back out to look for Cherry Blossom.

However, he could find no trace of his young wife. No one had seen her, until an old wandering beggar man, a pilgrim, came into the village seeking shelter for the night.

'Did you see a young woman on the road?' asked Yasunari.

'Yes,' said the old man. 'She was going towards the city. Are you her husband, Yasunari?'

'Yes!' he exclaimed, in astonishment.

'She gave me this message for you,' continued the old man. 'Tell Yasunari I have had to resume my journey to the temple. Do not try and follow me as it is decreed I must end my life there. Look after our son and bring him up to know that his mother's spirit will always return in the spring blossoms.'

Yasunari was distraught and left the next morning for the city in search of Cherry Blossom. But he never saw his beloved wife again nor heard any word of her fate. In later years, he always treasured the old pilgrim's words.

In the fullness of time, Yasunari and Cherry Blossom's baby son grew up to become a famous gardener. He travelled all over Japan designing gardens and, whichever plants and trees he chose, pride of place was always given to the flowering cherry.

Paradise Regained

Easter is associated with flowers, particularly the lily family, which includes what the Bible calls 'lilies of the field', such as bog asphodel and the fragile fritillaries, primroses, stately white hothouse lilies, bluebells, though these usually appear in May, and lily-of-the-valley.

Eastre was a Saxon goddess of spring. Christian celebrations, originally connected with the Jewish Passover, were deliberately aligned with these older customs to aid 'conversion'. The spring equinox is closely followed in the Christian calendar by Lady's Day, the Annunciation, on

25 March, and then Easter week. At one time, this marked the beginning of the year, a custom that Christianity has preserved.

Perhaps, though, what deeply connects Easter with flowers is the religious idea of Paradise. Gardens feature in most religions but are especially prominent in traditions that began in the Middle East. For Muslims, the heavenly Paradise is a garden, and for Islam, Judaism and Christianity, the divine Creator's perfect artwork is the first garden, Eden. That may be why the Christian resurrection also takes place in a garden on the first Easter Day.

However, the path from Eden to Easter is not smooth. After Adam and Eve were tricked by the serpent of the garden into eating the forbidden fruit, God commanded the angels to drive them out and to guard the entrances with a fiery sword.

At first Adam and Eve cowered in a place of gloom, darkness and cold, without food or shelter, for six days. They wept and lamented their fate. But on the seventh day the Creator took pity on them. He sent a guardian angel to lead the humans into a brighter, warmer land. The angel showed them trees and bushes from which they could gather fruit to eat. They were glad, for though this world could not compare to the paradise they had lost, they were no longer in darkness and could go on living.

Many years later, when Adam and Eve's son Seth had grown up, his father told him about Eden. 'This land is not our true home,' he told the boy. 'That was in the garden we had to leave, because we ate the forbidden fruit, and came to know about good and evil.'

Seth sensed his father's deep sadness at this loss, and he was very upset. He fasted for forty days and nights, and prayed to God to help his father, Adam. God too was moved, and he sent an angel to Seth with the branch of a tree from the garden. 'This is your father's comfort and his joy,' the angel said to Seth.

So, Seth brought the branch to Adam, saying, 'Father, this is a living branch from your true home.' And Adam looked at it with fear, for he saw that it was a branch from the tree of the knowledge of good and evil, which brought death.

'No, my son.' he said. 'This is the forbidden tree.'

'Once,' replied Seth, 'this tree brought death but now its gives light and life to this world.'

Time passed, and the human family flourished on earth. But still in his heart Adam felt the sadness of exile. When Seth's son Enoch grew up, he asked, 'Why is my grandfather sad?'

'Because,' Seth replied, 'he tasted the forbidden fruit and had to leave the garden of Eden.'

This troubled Enoch, who was pure and tender of heart. He fasted and prayed for forty days and nights, and then he began to plant a new garden on this earth, saying, 'The son must pay the debts of his father!' And Enoch filled the garden with every kind of flower and fruit, and he himself was filled with heavenly wisdom.

And Adam died, and Seth died, and Enoch lived on in his garden for many centuries, until one day, an angel plucked Enoch like a ripe pomegranate and placed him in Paradise, where he remains to this day.

But Enoch's gift continued through the generations and his garden multiplied and spread across the earth. And so it was that on Easter Day, Mary Magdalene, another Eve, came to the garden to mourn for the death of her beloved lord. But there she met the gardener, who was revealed to her once more as the divine creator:

> I got me flowers to straw Thy way,
> I got me boughs off many a tree;
> But Thou wast up by break of day,
> And brought'st Thy sweets along with Thee.

(George Herbert)

The Tulip Pixies

Once there was an old woman who lived in a small, white-washed cottage in a sheltered hollow right on the edge of town. At the back of the cottage was a vegetable garden, and at the front a flower garden, which was the old woman's pride and joy.

In every season of the year there were flowers in this garden. Even in January, the old woman had snowdrops, soon followed by yellow aconites and purple crocuses. As February went into March, she had primroses and violets, and then polyanthus and periwinkle. Then as spring warmed, she added daffy-down-dillies, wallflowers, pansies and forget-me-nots, soon to be followed by daisies, roses, pinks, campanulas, stocks, Canterbury bells and sweet Williams. And she loved every single flower, yet most of all, the old woman loved her tulips.

They grew along both sides of the path from her garden gate to the front door, and she would walk up and down watching for the green shoots to come through. Then she talked to the young plants, encouraging them to grow. 'All a-growing and a-blowing,' she hummed. 'Bless you, all a-growing and a-blowing.'

And indeed they were, opening their green leaves, forming buds and then opening up into pink, yellow, white and blue flowers. 'Pretty, pretty, my lovelies,' the old woman said. And indeed they were. By May, there was a full show of tulips, tall and strong, waving in the gentle breeze. These flowers were truly her pride and joy.

One night in May there was a full moon that shone, round and clear, over the garden, turning night into day. The old woman was going to bed when she thought, 'How pretty the tulips must look by moonlight.' So she opened the front door and peeped out. 'All a-growing and a-nodding,' she murmured. 'Bless you, all a-growing and a-nodding.' And she was just shutting the door, about to go to bed, when she heard soft music. What could it be?

So, the old woman went back onto the path, and walked to her gate. And still gentle music wafted through the warm air. But there was no sign of anyone in the garden or on the road. Then suddenly, she realised the music was coming from her flowers, the tulips.

'Bless me, my goodness,' whispered the old woman, and she stooped over the flowers. 'It's the pixies, they're singing for the May.' And she peeked into the first flower, and the second, and the third ... 'Bless me, bless me, my goodness' ... for in every flower there was a pixie baby sound asleep.

Well, of course, the pixies were out dancing in the moonlight and needed somewhere safe and soft for the babies to dream. The tulips were their cradles, rocking gently in the warm night air. 'Bless their little hearts,' thought the old woman, as she tiptoed back inside and went to bed. She was so pleased that the pixies had chosen her garden, and she slipped into the best sleep she had enjoyed for months.

Now, for a long, long time the old woman lived in her little white cottage and grew all her flowers. But however often she replanted or changed a flower, she always kept tulips on both sides of her front path from the garden gate to her front door. And every year, without fail, at May time, by night, the pixies placed their babies in her cradles so that they could dance in a ring. And the old woman fell asleep to the sound of their music.

MAY

The month begins with heraldic emblazons of colour. At the foot of the garden, pink apple blossom presides over a set piece of wild hyacinths, white and purple honesty, and an upsurge of irrepressible brunnera, whose intense blue star-shaped flowers are a hotspot for honeybees.

If only there was time to stop and learn to see, or paint directly from Nature. Human artistry lags behind her profusion and organic wit. As I stood gazing at this composition, a goldfinch landed beneath the apple tree, replete with its red and black helmet and its yellow surcoat. This little bird is called a 'gowd-spink' in Scotland and, today, he added a trumpet peal to my sun-kissed concerto.

Taking a higher view over adjacent walled gardens, there is an airy fanfare of cherry trees, fruited or ornamental, apple blossom, pear blossom, all undergirded by the first climbing ribbons of clematis. People are starting to sit out and even to venture for an early lunch alfresco.

In the nearby grounds of Prestonfield House, the peacocks are displaying their astonishing May colours. In India's Rajasthan, they herald the monsoon rains, restoring a parched landscape to fertile abundance. Traditional dancers imitate the peacock's glory with feathered costumes and choreographed mating displays. In the northern hemisphere it is the sun that presides over cycles of fertility, but in India it is the rain.

Do we still have garden rituals in Britain? Absolutely, though some are personal and linked to family memories of favourite flowers and childhood tasks. There is also the world of play that memory associates with green spaces and hiding places. But I still revel in my present-day ceremonies. As a member of a Mummers' group that turns out each May, I invariably go into our garden early on Beltane to gather fresh greenery and flowers. Then I decorate the timber frame and bamboo garlands that – after the ties have been tightened and all the straps checked – turn me into a kind of walking tree. A mummer prepares!

There is a moment of peaceful concentration and quiet before all the bustle of bells, dance and music. The last touch is always a branch of flowering hawthorn to deter any adverse spirits from spoiling such an auspicious day.

Hal-en Tow, Jolly Rumbelow
We are up long before the Day-O
To welcome in the morning
To welcome in the May-O
For summer is a comin' in
And we are to the green wood gone
To merry in the May-O.

Poets like Milton echo the mummers in more stately May mode:

> Now the bright morning-star, day's harbinger,
> Comes dancing from the east, and leads with her
> The flowery May, who from her green lap throws
> The yellow cowslip, and the pale primrose.
> Hail, bounteous May
> […]
> Thus we salute thee with our early Song,
> And welcome thee, and wish thee long.

However, May is work as well as play. There is a rush of activity in the vegetable garden with seedlings transplanted from greenhouse and cold frame into their growing positions. This is on-the-knees labour with finger touch on soil and tiny plants – a very satisfying contact with Mother Earth, the soul in the soil. In Scotland, direct sowing in April needs some form of cold-weather covering, but in May everything is suddenly possible and all the available ground fills up quickly.

Then there is the saga of my apple trees. I want to plant three where the rampant ivy has been uprooted and intersperse them with climbing roses. I have been researching native varieties, but now we are in coronavirus lockdown. I could send for specialist stock online, but this is not the right season for bare-rooted trees to take root. My dilemma is resolved by one of the community gardens, which is expanding its orchard and has surplus trees.

So, in return for a donation, I become the proud owner of two small Adam Pearmain apple trees, and one quince apple, all blossoming happily in large pots. They have been grown from cuttings taken from thriving trees in a Fife orchard. Such is the strength of the community garden networks.

Transplanting them becomes another May task, though one with decades of return ahead. All being well, they will outlive me, adding to Edinburgh's reputed 150,000 apple trees. 'Garden City' should be added to the city's accolades of 'Scotland's Capital', 'Festival City', and 'Queen of the North'. For now, Edina is the May Queen.

But this burst of activity succeeds four weeks of dry weather. Apart from a few non-eventful showers and one early May morning of rain, we have enjoyed unbroken blue skies. So, everything must be watered daily, in my own and in the community gardens.

No hoses are allowed; it is a watering can job – fill, pour, fill and pour again. There is a refreshing gush as cool water rushes into the empty can. Early mornings are a beautiful time for this job as thirsty earth breathes in sunrise air and moist dew.

The early summer evenings are also long now and mantled with peace, and a full moon rising. Other work must take its place within these diurnal rhythms. We are blessed by what is named in Japan the Flower Moon, the last supermoon of the year. Our weather is unusual and touched by magic, through a difficult period for human society.

After a relieving night of rain, there is a dash to plant out. Then inexplicably comes a final cold snap with two nights of sub-zero temperatures. Welcome to Scotland. The brakes go on and some seedlings are returned to the greenhouse, while sunny days gradually restore the equilibrium.

Is it this underlying cool that has made the swallows late to arrive this year? One friend reports a sighting near Duddingston, but as we know, one swallow does not make a summer. I take advantage of the planting lull to walk further afield and am rewarded with the spectacle of at least two dozen swifts hurtling over a waving field of green corn. Nearby is a fertiliser tower and a manure heap, and a river to provide the ready water they crave. What a display of speed and control to raise the spirit.

On the same outing I spot a kestrel being mobbed by three rooks. They dive bomb from above to protect their nests until the hawk rises effortlessly above them, going higher and higher beyond my vision.

Next there is a weekend of moderate rain. The vegetables begin some serious growth, and so do the weeds. But soon the mixed spell of weather gives way to sun. This moves us into what is called locally a 'drouth'. Watering becomes essential while the weeds need still more attention.

As May ends, two vigorous green sprays of oriental poppies burst into flower, morning by morning, in the border. The hard green buds open in a generous yet delicate goblet of orange petals. Inside their spread is a deep purple corona.

On the last day of May two male pheasants appear in the grass-land. They are clumsy movers, but their plumage is a spectrum of intense crimson, russet gold, emerald green and turquoise. These are our native peacocks, harbingers now of our short but vivid high summer.

In the absence of swallows, those skimming swifts have lingered in my mind, so I take a break to go back and see them again. Nothing – not a sign of swift life at that spot. Were the birds just scouting for a site to nest, or on an excursion to hoover up insects above the young crop, or just getting some exercise like me? Nature excels at these one-offs, and we scrabble to keep pace with her surprises. I am left grateful for that sighting, and my lingering sensation of shimmer and speed.

The Marriage of Bride

It is hard by May to remember that Bride,
goddess of spring, was locked fast in a
mountain, harshly imprisoned by her own
mother Beira, the old Cailleach of winter. And
that snow, sleet and hail were hurled across land and sea, as
the rocks were struck by Beira's hammer. After all, everything
is now green and growing.

But the story of Bride is not over. And what of Beira?
Eventually, despite calling up her storm hags, the Cailleach
was unable to resist the warm west winds coming in the wake
of golden-haired Angus Og from his island home. So, Beira
retreated to lie in frustrated fury on the Cuillins of Skye, where
the remnants of snow still lay. She was weak and exhausted.

But the Cailleach could not rest there. She dragged herself
down to the shore and crawled into a curragh, a little boat made
of wood and hide, and pushed herself out into the current. She
was carried far out west until the boat beached at the furthermost
landfall, the Isle of the Ever Young. And there Beira crept on her
hands and knees to the Well of Everlasting Life, and before expir-
ing, she touched her parched tongue with three drops of water
from the well. So, some say, she will be able to return in the next
cycle as Bride.

As for Bride, she has been walking through the land with
violets, primroses and bluebells flowering beneath her feet. And
in the glens, she met Angus Og, riding his fine white horse, displaying his crimson robe and long golden locks for all to admire.

'What kept you so long?' challenged Bride.

Angus dismounted and knelt before Bride to beg her favour.
And spring was betrothed to the promise of summer.

It is that promise that brings in Beltane, and a May wedding.
The plants bloom and the trees put out green leaves. Banners

flutter in a breeze alive with new life. The woods are carpeted with gold and purple and blue. And the Good People, the gentle kind, come riding in their dawn procession, clothed in green, with golden reins and silver bells. The whole land breathes peace and plenty.

Something of this woodland mystery permeates park and garden in May, inviting us to participate in Mary Webb's secret joy:

> Face to face with the sunflower,
> Cheek to cheek with the rose,
> We follow a secret highway
> Hardly a traveller knows.
> The gold that lies in the folded bloom
> Is all our wealth;
> We eat of the heart of the forest
> With innocent stealth.
> We know the ancient roads
> In the leaf of a nettle,
> And bathe in the blue profound
> Of a speedwell petal.

Poppy May *or* Thumbelina

There was once a woman who wanted to have a tiny, wee child, but she did not know where to find one. So, one day, she went to an old wise woman and said to her, 'I should so much like to have a tiny, wee child. Can you tell me where I can get one?'

'Oh, we have just got one ready!' said the wise woman. 'Here is a little seed for you. Put it in a flowerpot, and then you will see something happen.'

'Oh, thank you!' said the woman. Then she went home and planted the seed. Immediately there grew out of it a large and beautiful flower, which looked like a poppy, but the petals were tightly closed as if it were still only a bud.

'What a beautiful flower!' exclaimed the woman, and she kissed the closed petals; but as she kissed them the flower burst open. It was a real poppy, such as you can see in May, but in the middle of the large blossom, on the green velvety petals, sat a little girl, quite tiny and trim. She was scarcely half a thumb in height and so they called her Thumbelina.

An elegant, polished walnut shell served Thumbelina as a cradle, the blue petals of a violet were her mattress and a rose leaf her quilt. There she lay at night, but in the daytime, she used to play about on the table. Here the woman had put a bowl surrounded by a ring of flowers, with their stalks in water, in the middle of which floated a delicate poppy petal. On this Thumbelina sat and sailed from one side of the bowl to the other, rowing herself with two white horse hairs for oars. It was such a pretty sight! She could sing too, with a voice softer and sweeter than had ever been heard before.

One night, when she was lying in her little bed, an old toad crept in from the garden through an open window. She was ugly, clumsy and clammy; she hopped on to the table where Thumbelina lay asleep under the red rose leaf.

'This would make a beautiful wife for my son,' said the toad, taking up the walnut shell, with Thumbelina inside, and hopping with it through the window.

A wide stream flowed at the foot of the garden, with slippery and marshy banks. Here the toad lived with her son. Ugh! How ugly and clammy he was, just like his mother!

'Croak, croak, croak!' was all he could say when he saw the lovely little girl in the walnut shell.

'Don't talk so loud, or you'll wake her,' said the old toad. 'She might escape us even now; she is as light as a feather. We will put her at once on a broad water lily leaf in the stream. That will be quite an island for her; she is so small and light. She can't run away from us there, while we are preparing the hole under the marsh where she shall live.'

Outside in the brook grew many water lilies, with broad green leaves, which looked as if they were swimming about on the water. The leaf furthest away was the largest, and to this the old toad swam with Thumbelina in her walnut shell.

Tiny Thumbelina woke up very early in the morning, and when she saw where she was, she began to cry bitterly, for on every side of the great green leaf was water, and she could not get to the land.

The old toad was down under the marsh, decorating her room with rushes and yellow marigold leaves, to make it very grand for her new daughter-in-law. She swam out with her ugly son to the leaf where Thumbelina lay. She wanted to fetch the pretty cradle to put it into her room before Thumbelina herself came there. The old toad bowed low in the water before her, and said, 'Here is my son – you shall marry him and live in a fine chamber down under the marsh.'

'Croak, croak, croak,' was all that the son could say.

They took the neat little cradle and swam away with it, but Thumbelina sat alone on the great green leaf and wept, for she did not want to live with the clammy toad or marry her ugly son.

The little fishes swimming about under the water had seen the toad quite plainly and heard what she had said, so they put up their heads to see the little girl. When they saw her, they thought her so lovely that they were very sorry she should go down to live with the ugly toad. No, that must not happen. They assembled in the water around the green stalk that supported the leaf on which she was sitting, and nibbled the stem in two. Away floated the leaf down the stream, bearing Thumbelina far beyond the reach of the toad.

On she sailed, past several towns, and the little birds sitting in the bushes saw her, and sang, 'What a lovely little girl!' The leaf floated farther and farther away, and so Thumbelina left her northern land.

A beautiful white butterfly fluttered above her and at last settled on the leaf. Thumbelina pleased him, and she too was delighted, for now the toads could not reach her, and it was so beautiful where she was travelling – the sun shone on the water and made it sparkle like the brightest silver.

A great chaffinch came flying past. He caught sight of Thumbelina, and in a moment had put his arms around her slender waist and had flown off with her to a tree. The green leaf floated away down the stream and the butterfly with it. How terrified poor Thumbelina was when the chaffinch flew off with her to the tree!

But the chaffinch did not trouble himself about that. He sat down with her on a large green leaf, gave her the honey out of the flowers to eat, and told her that she was very pretty, although she wasn't in the least like a chaffinch. Later on, all the other chaffinches who lived in the same tree came to pay calls. They examined Thumbelina closely, and remarked, 'How very miserable!'

'How ugly she is!' Said all the lady chaffers – and yet Thumbelina was very pretty. The chaffinch who had stolen her knew this very well but when he heard all the ladies saying she was ugly, he began to think so too, and would not keep her; she might go wherever she liked. So, he flew down from the tree with her and put her on a daisy. There she sat and wept, because she was so ugly that the chaffinch would have nothing to do with her, and yet she was the most beautiful creature imaginable, so soft and delicate, like the loveliest rose leaf.

The whole summer poor wee Thumbelina lived alone in the great wood. She plaited a bed for herself from blades of grass and hung it up under a clover leaf, so that she was protected from the rain; she gathered honey from the flowers for food and drank the dew on the leaves every morning.

Thus, the summer and autumn passed, but then came winter – the long, cold winter. All the birds who had sung so sweetly about her had flown away; the trees shed their leaves; the flowers died and the great clover leaf under which she had lived curled up, and nothing remained of it but the withered stalk. She was terribly cold, for her clothes were ragged, and she herself was so small and thin.

Poor little Thumbelina! She would surely be frozen to death. It began to snow, and every snowflake that fell on her was to her as a whole shovelful thrown on one of us, for we are so big, and she was only an inch high. She wrapped herself up in a dead leaf, but it was torn in the middle and gave her no warmth; she was trembling with cold.

Just outside the wood where she was now living lay a great cornfield, but the corn had been gone a long time and only the dry, bare stubble was left standing in the frozen ground. This made a forest for her to wander about in. All at once, she came across the door of a field mouse, who had a little hole under a corn stalk. There the mouse lived warm and snug, with a store-room full of corn and a splendid kitchen and dining room.

Poor little Thumbelina went up to the door and begged for a little piece of barley, for she had not had anything to eat for the last two days.

'Poor little creature!' said the field mouse, for she was a kind-hearted old thing. 'Come into my warm room and have some dinner with me.'

And she was so pleased with Thumbelina, she said, 'As far as I am concerned you may spend the winter with me; but you must keep my room clean and tidy, and tell me stories, for I like that very much.'

Thumbelina did everything that the kind old field mouse asked and did it wonderfully well.

'Now I am expecting a visitor,' said the field mouse. 'My neighbour comes to call on me once a week. He is better off than I am, has great big rooms, and wears a fine black velvet coat. If you could only marry him, you would be well provided for – but he is blind. You must tell him all the prettiest stories you know.'

But Thumbelina did not trouble her head about him, for he was only a mole. He came and paid them a visit in his black velvet coat.

'He is so rich and so accomplished,' the old field mouse told her. 'His house is twenty times larger than mine. He has great knowledge, but he cannot bear the sun and the beautiful flowers, and speaks slightingly of them, for he has never seen them.'

Thumbelina had to sing to the mole, so she sang, 'Ladybird, ladybird, fly away home!' and other songs so prettily that the mole fell in love with her. But he did not say anything as he was very cautious.

A short time before, he had dug a long passage through the ground from his own house to that of his neighbour. He gave the field mouse and Thumbelina permission to walk in it as often as they liked. He begged them not to be afraid of the dead bird that lay in the passage – it was a real bird, with beak and feathers, and must have died a little time ago, and now laid buried just where he had made his tunnel.

The mole took a piece of rotten wood in his mouth, for that glows like fire in the dark, and went in front, lighting them through the long, dark passage. When they came to the place where the dead bird lay, the mole put his broad nose against the ceiling and pushed a hole through, so that the daylight could shine down.

In the middle of the path lay a dead swallow, his pretty wings pressed close to his sides, his claws and head drawn under his feathers. The poor bird had evidently died of the cold. Thumbelina was very sorry, for she was very fond of all little birds; they had sung and twittered so beautifully to her all through the summer.

But the mole kicked him with his bandy legs and said, 'Now he can't sing anymore! It must be very miserable to be a little bird! I'm thankful that none of my little children are. Birds like this one always starve in winter.'

'Yes, you speak like a sensible man,' said the field mouse. 'What has a bird, in spite of all his singing, in the wintertime? He must starve and freeze, and that must be very pleasant for him, I don't think!'

Thumbelina did not say anything, but when the other two had passed on she bent down to the bird, brushed aside the feathers from his head, and kissed his closed eyes gently. 'Perhaps it was he who sang to me so prettily in the summer,' she thought. 'How much pleasure he gave me, dear little bird!'

The mole closed up the hole again and then escorted the ladies home. But Thumbelina could not sleep that night, so she got out of bed and plaited a great big blanket of straw and carried it off, spread it over the dead bird, and piled upon it thistledown as soft as cotton wool, which she had found in the field mouse's room, so that the poor little thing should lie warmly buried.

'Farewell, lovely little bird!' she said. 'Farewell – and thank you for your beautiful songs in the summer, when the trees were green and the sun shone down warmly on us!' Then she laid her head against the bird's heart.

But the bird was not dead. He had been frozen, but now that she had warmed him, his heart was beating once more. He was coming to life. In autumn the swallows fly away to foreign lands, but there are some who are late in starting, and then they get so cold that they drop down as if dead, and the snow comes and covers them over.

Thumbelina trembled, she was so frightened as the bird was very large in comparison with herself, only an inch high. But she took courage, piled up the down more closely over the poor swallow, fetched her own quilt and laid it over his head.

Next night, she crept out again to him. There he was, alive but very weak; he could only open his eyes for a moment to look at Thumbelina, who was standing in front of him with a piece of rotten wood in her hand, for she had no other lantern.

'Thank you, little one,' said the swallow to her. 'Now I am so beautifully warm! Soon I shall regain my strength, and then I shall be able to fly out again into the sunshine.'

'It is very cold outside,' she said. 'It is snowing and freezing! Stay in your warm bed – I will take care of you!'

Then she brought him water in a petal, which he drank, and he told her how he had torn one of his wings on a bramble, so that he could not fly as fast as the other swallows, who had flown far away to warmer lands. He had dropped down exhausted, and then he could remember no more.

The whole winter he remained down there, and Thumbelina looked after him and nursed him tenderly. Neither the mole nor the field mouse heard anything about this, for they could not bear the poor swallow.

When the spring came and the sun warmed the earth again, the swallow said farewell to Thumbelina, who opened the hole in the roof for him that the mole had made. The sun shone brightly down upon her, and the swallow asked her if she would go with him – she could sit upon his back. Thumbelina wanted very much to fly far away into the green wood, but she knew that the old field mouse would be sad if she ran away. 'No, I mustn't come!' she said.

'Farewell, dear good little girl!' said the swallow, and flew off into the sunshine. Thumbelina gazed after him with the tears standing in her eyes, for she was very fond of the swallow. 'Tweet, tweet,' sang the bird, and flew into the green wood.

'Now you are to be a bride, Thumbelina!' said the field mouse, 'For our neighbour has proposed to you! What a piece of fortune for a poor child like you! You must set to work at your linen for your marriage, for nothing must be lacking when summer is passed if you are to become the wife of our neighbour, the mole!'

But she was not at all pleased, for she did not like the stupid mole. Every morning when the sun was rising, and every evening when it was setting, she would steal outside, and when the breeze parted the ears of corn so that she could see the blue sky through them, she thought how bright and beautiful it must be outside, and longed to see her dear swallow again. But he never came; no doubt he had flown away far into the great green wood.

By the autumn Thumbelina had finished all the clothes and linen for her wedding. 'In four weeks, you will be married!' said the field mouse. 'Don't be obstinate, or I shall bite you with my sharp white teeth! You will get a fine husband! The king himself has not such a velvet coat. His storeroom and cellar are full, and you should be thankful.'

Well, the wedding day arrived. The mole had come to fetch Thumbelina to live with him deep down under the ground, never to come out into the warm sun again, for that was what he didn't like. The poor little girl was very sad for now she must say goodbye to the beautiful sun.

'Farewell, bright sun!' she cried, stretching out her arms towards it, and taking another step outside the house, for now the corn had been reaped and only the dry stubble was left standing. 'Farewell, farewell,' she said, and put her arms around a little red flower that grew there. 'Give my love to the dear swallow when you see him!'

'Tweet, tweet!' sounded in her ear all at once.

She looked up. There was the swallow flying past! As soon as he saw Thumbelina, he was very glad. She told him how unwilling she was to marry the ugly mole, as she would have to live underground where the sun never shone, and she could not help bursting into tears.

'The cold winter is coming now,' said the swallow, 'and I must fly away to warmer lands. Will you come with me? You can sit on my back, and we will fly far away from the ugly mole and his dark house, over the mountains, to the warm countries where the sun shines more brightly than here, where it is always summer, and there are always beautiful flowers. Do come with me, dear little Thumbelina, who saved my life when I lay frozen in the dark tunnel!'

'Yes, yes I will go with you,' said Thumbelina, and got on the swallow's back, with her feet on one of his outstretched wings. Up he flew into the air, over woods and seas, over the great mountains where the snow is always lying. If she was cold, she crept under his warm feathers, only keeping her little head out to admire all the beautiful things in the world beneath.

At last, they came to warm lands; there, the sun was brighter, the sky seemed twice as high, and in the hedges hung the finest green and purple grapes. In the woods grew oranges and lemons; the air was scented with myrtle and mint, and on the roads were pretty little children running about and playing with great gorgeous butterflies.

But the swallow flew on farther, and it became more and more beautiful. Under the most splendid green trees besides a blue lake stood a glittering white-marble castle. Vines hung about the high pillars; there were many swallows' nests, and in one of these lived the swallow who was carrying Thumbelina.

'Here is my house!' he said, 'but it won't do for you to live with me; I am not tidy enough. You will find a home for yourself in one of the lovely flowers that grow down there. Now I will set you down, and you can do whatever you like.'

'Splendid!' said Thumbelina, clapping her hands.

There below lay a great white marble column that had fallen to the ground and broken into three pieces, but between these grew the most beautiful white flowers. The swallow flew down with Thumbelina and set her upon one of the broad leaves. To her astonishment, she found a tiny little man sitting in the middle of the flower, as white and transparent as if he were made of glass. He had the loveliest golden crown on his head and the most beautiful wings on his shoulders. He himself was no bigger than Thumbelina. He was the flower spirit. In each blossom there dwelt a tiny man or woman; but this one was the king over the others.

'How handsome he is,' whispered Thumbelina to the swallow.

The little prince was very frightened of the swallow for, in comparison with one so tiny as himself, the bird seemed a giant. But when he saw Thumbelina he was delighted, for she was the most beautiful girl he had ever seen.

He took his golden crown off his head and put it on hers, asking her name, and if she would be his wife – then she would be queen of all the flowers.

Yes! He was a different kind of husband to the son of the toad and the mole with the black velvet coat. She said, 'Yes,' to the noble prince.

Out of each flower came a lady and gentleman, each so tiny and pretty that it was a pleasure to see them. Each brought Thumbelina a present, but the best of all was a beautiful pair of wings that were fastened on to her back so she too could fly from flower to flower. They all wished her joy, and the swallow sat above in his nest and sang the 'Wedding March', and that he did as well as he could. But he was sad, because he was very fond of Thumbelina and did not want to be separated from her.

'You shall not be called Thumbelina!' said the flower spirit. 'That is a horrid name, and you are far too lovely for that. We will call you Poppy May.'

'Farewell, farewell!' said the little swallow with a heavy heart, and flew away to farther lands, far, far away, right back to the north. There he had a nest above a window in the garden shed, where his wife lived. 'Tweet, tweet,' he sang to her.

She can tell fairy stories. And that is the way we learned the whole tale of Thumbelina, or as she became, Poppy May.

Five Queens

Can one garden have five queens? Let me tell you about the community garden that does – and that is just so far. There is Queen Beatrix, who is a Queen Mum with two daughters, Queens Marjory I, who left to form a new queendom, and Marjory II. Otherwise, we would have had six majesties instead of five. Then there is Queen Mary, who succeeded Beatrix. Lastly come Queens Hazel and Kirsten, who are not related to Beatrix or to each other.

Of course, everyone has seen huge bumblebees buzzing round the garden in spring. They are all young queens looking for somewhere to build their nest. If they succeed, they will reign over their worker bees for one summer. At the end of the season, they lay eggs to produce next year's queens.

But our five queens are the much more powerful honeybees. Each one reigns over a whole hive of workers, thousands of them, who make lovely golden honey to put on bread or scones, or in sweet puddings and warm, soothing drinks.

Where would we be without honey? And what is the secret magic in honey that gives humans health and happiness? It is the very essence of the sun gathered by these clever airborne insects.

Each of our queens – Beatrix, then Mary, Marjory, Hazel and Kirsten – have a palace made of wax built inside a wooden hut or hive. All the worker bees live there and many of them fly out daily to gather pollen, which is like gold dust, and nectar, which is like syrup from the flowers. While doing this they move pollen from flower to flower, which helps make more flowers and fruit. Then they bring their treasures of gold dust and syrup back to their hives to feed the queen's children.

The queen does not go out but lays lots of eggs that hatch into little grubs. Some of her worker bees also stay at home to make wax cells for each of the grubs. Next, they turn into stay-at-home bees, and when they are fed with nectar and pollen, they make honey, by washing the nectar round their mouths and then spitting it out! Then their wax homes turn into a honeycomb. If only we could make honey from mouthwash.

Busy bees! And sometimes the worker bees dance in the hive to show where they found the best food – 'Fly out,' they buzz. 'Fly out sisters, to fetch more sun food in!' They fizz with energy.

But apart from laying all her eggs, the honeybee queen has another great task to undertake. This is her marriage flight, the greatest event in her whole reign. Early the following summer, on a day she chooses, the queen will leave her hive, taking lots of the worker bees with her in a great swarm. This happens because the hive has become overcrowded and her bees may become ill. Bravely, the queen sets out to form a new hive, leaving one of her daughters to become the new queen.

At first her cloud, or swarm, of followers settles on a tree or bush. Scouts are sent out to find a new site for a hive. Fortunately, beekeepers are often on hand to coax the swarm gently (you don't want to annoy a swarm of bees) into a wide net and take them to an empty hive. There, they can begin life all over again, like migrants or refugees given a warm welcome in their new country.

Yet this can be a dangerous time for honeybee queens and their followers. When our Queen Beatrix's daughter, Marjory I, set out on her flight she was unable to lay any eggs in the new hive. So, her sister Marjory II had to set out on her marriage flight to save the new hive. Fortunately, everyone is doing well there now, and 6,000 eggs have been laid.

Meanwhile, in the first hive, Queen Mary had succeeded her mother Beatrix, who was ready to retire. In the community garden, they call the first hive 'Caberfeigh', and the new one 'Sunnybrae'.

The third hive in our garden, called 'Fairylea', was made when beekeepers brought a swarm that had landed in the garden of a nearby house that had no hive. Nobody knows where that marriage flight set out from, but it was led by Queen Hazel, who is very happy to be looked after in her new home by friendly gardeners and beekeepers. She and all her workers are thriving.

But the fourth hive, 'Old Manse', had a more dramatic beginning. A swarm of bees arrived unexpectedly outside a hotel in the centre of town. They called the beekeepers for help and they brought the stranded swarm to our garden. But the bees were in shock from the experience of being lost. They rejected their own queen, who died before anyone could give her a name. Now all the bees were in danger of dying before they could build up their new hive and make honey.

Then the beekeepers were called to a new garden swarm in Portobello. They brought these bees with their queen and put them in a box beside the bees who had been lost. Between the two swarms, they put a double sheet of newspaper. Gradually the bees nibbled through the paper. They became used to each other and to the smell of the Portobello queen. What a relief.

They all joined together as one, under one queen, now named Kirsten. These days, the Old Manse is one of the busiest hives in the community garden. Hurrah for Queen Kirsten!

What wonderful honey we can look forward to tasting. Admittedly, though, unlike our five queens and their busy workers, the male bees are rather lazy. As you may imagine, not many of them are needed, but they do hatch out later in the summer, after most of the hard work is done. Then they mate with the hive queen so there will be new queens next year, new swarms and new hives.

But in the marriage flight of the honeybee there is no king, only a queen. And that is the story of Beatrix, Marjory, Mary, Hazel and Kirsten. The Five Queens. May we never run out of bees and honey!

JUNE

It cannot possibly be the month of midsummer; this is far too soon. In Scotland, at least, despite a dry April, we have only had one month of summer so far, and hopefully two more lie ahead. With a bit of luck, we could still be sunning in September.

Nonetheless, these four weeks bring spectacular growth. With maximum light, sun and ample showers, everywhere exhibits abundance – borders, vegetable beds and herb pots. The insects multiply, from beneficent bees to the omnivorous cabbage fly. The birds are breeding, feeding and singing from early dawn to delayed dusk, as if there might be no tomorrow.

Quite casually, I encounter a wonder at the marshy little pond, close to the community garden. It seems to be alive – a mass of insects? No, it is one black, moving orgy of tadpoles. How many thousand frogs will each square metre yield? In the commonplace lurks the extraordinary. The nearby heronry will be gorged.

June is the month to crown that long-meditated project. First, the uprooting of the old ivy-choked shrubbery was hard, sweated labour. Then the planting of the apple trees. And now the rambling roses that will go behind them creating a new southern border for the garden – a year-round cycle of blossom and foliage.

The apples were a Scots sourcing, but England is the paradise of roses, with traditional stock and the careful cultivation of new varieties. We owe a lot to botanists, but even more to practical husbandry over many generations in our island nations. My choices are Gertrude Jekyll, a tribute rose bred by David Austin in honour of that most creative of all of England's garden designers. Then there is Rambling Rector, a prolific climber with a sharp hint of prolix pulpits. Then there is the yellow Pilgrim Rose, named for Chaucer's *Canterbury Tales*, and finally Veilchenblau, a reminder that no vainglorious Brexit rhetoric can uproot us from our shared European roots.

We are still in coronavirus lockdown this month, and one side benefit is long walks upriver to the Pentland Hills, and downriver as far as the Firth of Forth. Gradually, I accumulate stones to form a low wall – a drystane dyke – to separate the vegetable terrace from the apple trees and roses. I realise that even in this home terrain there is abundant geological variety; my wall turns eclectic depending on each passing day's direction of travel.

One day watering, then one of showers. One morning a stray lesser-spotted woodpecker is pecking at our telegraph pole; one evening a squirrel, denied birdseed by our neighbour's ingenious new feeders, voraciously raids my young cherry tree instead. So, the little tree must be staked and netted. And canes must also be crossed and tied to support the suddenly climbing beans.

Then equally suddenly June has gone. Did we miss the solstice?

Say it with Flowers

There is a language of flowers that seems
to reach far back in time. As a poet familiar
with folk tradition and close to the medieval
world, Shakespeare often evokes the symbolism
of flowers, as in Ophelia's strange lament:

> There's rosemary, that's for remembrance;
> pray you, love, remember: and there is pansies,
> that's for thoughts … There's fennel for you, and
> columbines: there's rue for you: and here's some
> for me: we may call it herb of grace o' Sundays: O you
> must wear your rue with a difference. There's a daisy: I
> would give you some violets, but they withered all when
> my father died.

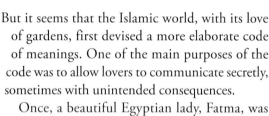

But it seems that the Islamic world, with its love
of gardens, first devised a more elaborate code
of meanings. One of the main purposes of the
code was to allow lovers to communicate secretly,
sometimes with unintended consequences.

Once, a beautiful Egyptian lady, Fatma, was
neglected by her husband, who had taken a
second wife. But attending the mosque, her
eye was caught by a handsome young artist
who was living in Cairo and painting its fine
buildings. She sent him a bouquet of carefully
selected flowers.

The painter, who was European, was puzzled
at receiving these flowers, but on the advice of
his servant he took them to an old lady, who
could read the message.

'My son,' she told the painter, 'this is a simple note, but from its elegance of style it is easy to see that the author is a woman of the first merit.' And she translated. 'You come each day to draw the mosque with its coloured stones. I watch you with pleasure concentrating on your work. I envy the cupola and the minaret because you gaze on them incessantly.'

The painter was astonished, but there was more to come. The old lady proceeded to convey a frank and whole-hearted declaration of love! 'Not being able to speak to you with my lips, I write with flowers. This bouquet is a message from my soul. May its intense colours, its symmetry, and its perfumes be an emblem of she who loves you.'

Being an artist, and highly susceptible, the young painter fell deeply in love with his mysterious correspondent. He had thought Paris the centre of amorous liberation. However, he could not identify his lover among the many veiled women at the mosque. With the help of the experienced older lady, he continued the correspondence.

Fatma, too, entered into the exchange with increasing emotion. The bouquets passed to and fro, with ever more passionate declarations. Both lovers retained their bouquets, he in his studio, she in her innermost chamber, so they could fondly trace the progress of their love.

Then one day, unexpectedly, the absent husband visited his wife's boudoir, and was horrified by the long line of preserved bouquets. He rushed out for an interpreter.

And so Fatma sent her final message.

'My dear friend, I am about to die. At midnight, when the moon will be bathing our city in her light, I shall be thrown into the Nile. We shall meet each other in another life, where we can continue our correspondence.'

Whether this was a final floral farewell, or a broad hint, or both, is unknown, but according to the tale, the painter rescued

Fatma, who had been tied in a sack, along with a cat and a viper, and carried her off to Paris.

Thus, the story goes, the formal language of flowers came to Europe.

It is true, as Jean Marsh observes in her lovely edition of Kate Greenaway's *Language of Flowers*, that as the nineteenth century progressed, a fashion for elaborate flower messaging took hold, though usually with more decorous intentions. Of course, the tale of Fatma's amorous floral designs is itself a product of Europeans imagining the 'oriental' as exotic and alluring.

Whatever the twists and turns of cultural codes, we are still fond of 'saying it with flowers', whether the message is one of love, sympathy or gratitude.

A Midsummer Dream?

Are there fairies at the bottom of the garden? This question much occupied the creator of Sherlock Holmes, Arthur Conan Doyle, whose devotion to psychic research led him to believe that the supposed photographs of the Cottingley fairies were genuine. By comparison, J.M. Barrie's discovery of Peter Pan in Kensington Gardens seems more calculated and knowing.

Of course, the Cottingley apparitions were what might be called 'flowery' fairies – winged, blossomy and petite. Sometimes Shakespeare's *A Midsummer Night's Dream*, with its Peasebottom, Mustardseed and Cobweb, gets blamed for creating these winged effervescents, but that is more the legacy of subsequent illustrators. In reality, Shakespeare's Puck or Robin Goodfellow is much closer to the fairy folk of British and Irish lore.

In whatever physical scale these creatures appear – and there is a wide spectrum – they are always chancy, and people must be very careful not to offend them. In Ireland, the fairies are 'on the other side' and therefore different from us in their emotions, or lack of them, and their values. They may do you a good turn and give you a gift, or they may turn against you and wreak havoc. Their gifts or blessings may be double edged.

In Scotland, speaking the 'f-word' is ill advised: much better you should refer to 'the little people', 'the wee folk' or 'the good people'. Just to be on the safe side.

Shakespeare's Puck or Robin Goodfellow is clearly in this category. As Charles Lamb has it, 'Puck was a shrewd and knavish sprite', who would prevent the milk churning into butter, spoil the ale, capsize drinks, tip up stools and generally wreak mischief on unsuspecting humans. But Shakespeare adds his own touch of natural magic to this everyday prankster, which comes closer to the mythic side of fairy lore:

Where the bee sucks, there suck I:
In a cowslip's bell I lie;
There I couch when owls do cry.
On the bat's back I do fly
After summer merrily,
Merrily, merrily shall I live now
Under the blossom that hangs on the bough.

Such magic is intimately connected with the virtues or 'humours' of plants, and the whole mad confusion of this midsummer night is set in train by the juice of a common pansy, ingeniously and mischievously applied at the command of Oberon, king of the fairies:

Yet marked I where the bolt of Cupid fell:
It fell upon a little western flower,
Before milk-white, now purple with love's wound,
And maidens call it love-in-idleness.

> Fetch me that flower; the herb I showed thee once.
> The juice of it on sleeping eyelids laid
> Will make man or woman madly dote
> Upon the next living creature that it sees.
> Fetch me this herb; and be thou here again
> Ere the leviathan can swim a league.

Powerful magic indeed, but not infallible if applied to the wrong pair of eyes! Puck claims it was an honest mistake …

Shakespeare revels in the exuberant night that ensues, packing it with all his favourite devices – mistaken identity, crossed purposes, disguise, mumming and madness. He keeps humour to the fore in his night of magical transformations, yet it is not hard to detect potentially sinister undertones. What if the magic is harmful or ill intended? One of the flowers attending on Titania, the fairy queen, is the apparently innocuous cowslip:

> The cowslips tall her pensioners be:
> In their gold coats spots you see.
> Those be rubies, fairy favours,
> In those freckles live their savours.

There was a persistent superstition against bringing a first primrose or cowslip from the garden into the house. This was an ill omen. Likewise, it was believed unlucky to gather a single or small bunch of these flowers and bring them indoors. Such beliefs could be turned against people in the form of ill wishings and curses.

In Lincolnshire, the tale was told of the girl who was sickly and struggled to get out of her bed. However, she was able with some help to go to the door take part in the ritual of bread and salt. The villagers would cast handfuls of bread and salt on their fields and gardens in the early months of the year, to avert any sickness or death arising from the green mists that covered the fens.

The girl dreamed of being able to be up and about gathering flowers in springtime, and so it transpired. She appeared much better, though sometimes tired and wan at the end of the day. She went visiting and danced and played with her friends.

In April, when the weather turned dry, the villagers took water to the fields and poured it into the four corners to bring rain. The girl went with them – the life and soul of the party. In May, she seemed to grow strangely beautiful. She took to watering the cowslips by the garden gate and dancing around them in the sunlight.

'Stop that!' said her mother. 'Leave them alone.'

'If you want me gone, mother,' said the girl, 'don't ever pick one of these flowers.'

The mother bit her tongue. 'They'll fade soon enough,' was all she said.

'Aye, they'll fade soon enough,' echoed her daughter.

One evening, a boy from the village stopped at the garden gate to chat with the girl and her mother. There was no special news, just the usual Fens gossip about weather, the dykes and the bogles. As they chatted, the boy idly picked a flower and twirled it in his fingers. As he turned to go, he dropped it without thinking.

'Did you pick that cowslip?' asked the girl, suddenly noticing.

'Aye,' said the lad, and bending down he picked up the flower and gave it to her. 'Here, it's yours.' And off he went, whistling cheerfully.

The girl stared at the flower and turned deathly white. Then, with a low moan, she fled up the garden path into her house. There she took to her bed. And in the morning, she was found white and shrunken, with the withered cowslip clasped tight in her dead hand.

Not Kissing the Frog

The garden sloped down to a lazy, meander-ing river, full of shallows and reed beds in the summer. At the top of the slope was a sturdily built stone house, surrounded by flower beds, a shed, a cold store and a barn where swallows nested every year. On the slope itself were vegeta-bles and a small orchard.

One fine evening, two days before midsummer, the lassie of the house stepped out to take the air. It was balmy, with flowers nodding in a gentle breeze, insects hovering and swallows gracefully swooping to fetch supper for themselves and a brood of hungry chicks.

At the river edge frogs had been hatching from thousands of eggs embedded in their spawn jelly. For herself, the girl favoured the newts, who are much more particular, wrapping every single egg in a leaf and sometimes carrying them in their mouth, until the leaf unfurls and the tadpole hatches, ready to swim out of its own accord.

Perhaps the lassie, too, was ready to start out in life of her own accord, or perhaps the restful warmth of the evening made her lazy and content. Either way, as she turned to stroll along the river bank, she encountered a full-grown frog. He was opening and closing his mouth and shooting out his long, viscous tongue between slobbery lips.

'It's a fine evening, lassie.'

She stared at the frog's bulging eyes in disbelief.

'Aye, I'm talking. Will you marry me?'

The eyes gleamed, and the girl laughed aloud. 'This is crazy. Why should I marry a creature like you?'

'Well, I didn't ask you to kiss me,' croaked the frog complacently. 'What do you say to honourable wedlock?'

'Shall I give my promise to a frog?'

'Why not?

'Oh well, yes, then, why not, indeed. I'll marry you,' giggled the lassie, derisively.

No further word was spoken. The frog hopped back into the river, leaving the lassie wondering at the tricks played on this midsummer night by her own eyes and ears. Then she shrugged it off and went back home, where she sat on the other side of the hearth from her mother, sewing a hem for her own new linen dress.

And so the next day passed, and the one after that, till the third evening, which was midsummer. As usual, the girl was at the fireside, working with her mother. Suddenly, there was a scraping and scratching at the door, and a harsh voice croaked outside:

Open the door, my hinny, my heart,

Open the door my true love;

Remember the promise that you and I made,

Down in the garden where we two met.

'Hoots,' said the mother. 'What's that at the door?'

'It's just a filthy paddo,' said the girl. 'Pay it no heed.'

'Ach, the poor paddo,' said the mother. 'Let the wee creature into the hearth.'

So, the girl got up reluctantly and unlatched the door. And the frog hopped over the stone floor and settled himself between the two wooden seats.

'That's better,' said the mother. 'You'll be more homely there.'

The frog burped contentedly and then opened his blubbery mouth wide:

Give me my supper, my hinny, my heart,
Give me my supper, my own true love;
Remember the promise that you and I made,
Down in the garden where we two met.

'I'll fetch no supper for that filthy wee paddo,' said the lassie.

'Ach, the poor paddo,' said the mother. 'Get him something to his supper. The wee soul must be starving.'

So, the girl got up reluctantly and fetched the frog a dish of oat mash with eggs folded in. He lapped it up greedily with his long tongue.

Then the frog burped again contentedly, and opened his blubbery mouth wide:

Put me to bed, my hinny, my heart,
Put me to bed, my own true love;
Remember the promise that you and I made,
Down in the garden where we two met.

'I'll touch no bedsheet belonging that slobbery, slimy wee creature,' pronounced the girl, putting her foot down firmly at last.

'Ach,' said the mother, 'you don't need to lie with the creature. Just lay the poor soul to rest like any Christian. Why don't you?'

In a fit of pique, the girl got up and threw open the bedroom door. The frog hopped over the stone floor and through the door. Then he jumped in one single leap into the nearest bed, which was the lassie's own.

'What a loup the wee creature has on him,' exclaimed the mother, admiringly.

Ensconced amidst the covers, the frog burped contentedly once more, and opened his blubbery mouth wide:

Fetch me an axe, my hinny, my heart,
Fetch me an axe, my own true love;
Remember the promise that you and I made,
Down in the garden where we two met.

Well, the lassie wasted no time in fetching an axe. But then she stood uncertainly in the doorway.

'Hoots,' cried the mother, 'what's got into the wee creature's head?'

But the frog stretched out his neck and sent his tongue in and out of his blubbery mouth at a rapid rate. Then he burped and croaked:

Chop off my head, my hinny, my heart,
Chop off my head, my own true love;
Remember the promise that you and I made,
Down in the garden where we two met.

The girl closed her eyes and swung the axe.

The mother screamed.

The frog burped for the last time.

All fell deathly silent.

The girl opened her eyes to see a handsome young man standing on the stone flags before her.

'Thank you, fine lass,' he said. 'You have freed me from a wicked spell. Will you truly marry me?'

The mother fainted clean away.

The girl opened her slender lips, and said in a sweet but firm voice:

Give me your hand, my hinny, my heart,
Give me your hand, my own true love;
Remember the promise that you and I made,
Down in the garden where we two met.

The handsome prince, for surely he must have been a prince to fall under such enchantment, sank to his knees before her. And she leaned down graciously and kissed him gently on the lips.

And as the tale was told to me, they all lived happy and never drank out of a dry cappy.

JULY

Showery rain alternates with shining sun. It is warm but not hot, and watering becomes an occasional supplement through drier spells. Light is rinsed, cleansed and colours vibrate.

Looking across the community garden is like surveying a roughshod Eden. Red climbing beans and yellow sunflowers, wild lilac poppies and white flowering brassicas, green leaves and scarlet berries, compete for attention.

The growth surge is phenomenal, above and below ground. It is easy to be seduced by the primary visuals and forget the teeming universe of insects and worms. The ants do sterling work, digging and cleaning; spiders and moths help our birds reduce the plant-destroying grubs and slugs; ladybirds and lacewings consume countless aphids. But the true heroes of any garden are the anonymous earthworms, who ceaselessly enrich our soil.

Some benighted souls find worms boring, but they do not include children, or Charles Darwin who spent years directly observing them.

Worms eat soil, the more organic the better, and then void earth rich in nutrients and minerals. They are also inveterate and strongly muscled tunnellers, aerating the soil around plant roots and producing nitrates. In the process, worms push finer earth to the surface, sinking stones and gravel over time, in an underground version of ploughing. Moreover, they continue this work twelve months of the year, going deeper to escape winter cold, though some species tunnel down to sleep in burrows.

Moreover, worms enjoy a rich sex life. Each adult worm has both male and female sex organs, but they need to mate with each other to produce eggs. To do this, they lie close together for an extended period, covering themselves with mucus and exchanging sperm. Both partners store sperm in a sac, lay eggs and then fertilise them, by wriggling backwards out of a membrane collar that retains some of the sperm. The richer the soil, the more prolific the worms become. In this case, an orgy generates a virtuous circle of fertility. Much of this is, of course, invisible below ground, but exploring an active compost bin in all seasons quickly reveals this teeming energy of life.

The compost bin also needs plant matter and ideally food waste. There are plenty of both in July alongside the fast-growing weeds. This, however, divides gardeners. Some seek a weed-free paradise, and keep perennial weeds out of their compost. Others echo Gerard Manley Hopkins' cry, 'Long live the weeds and the wilderness yet!'

Of course, weeds are just plants in what is perceived to be 'the wrong place', so somewhere a balance must be struck between growing to eat and providing an ideal ecosystem for insects, birds and small mammals. I let the weeds come on and then harvest them for worm-producing compost with which to build up the vegetable beds. Virtuous circles – no inorganic fertilisers involved.

Many gardeners, though, stop short of celebrating tough-rooted spreaders. Bindweed, for example, will choke anything in time, despite its pretty white blossoms, but in my view nettles

and dandelions deserve areas of refuge. For centuries they were welcomed as plants with healing properties, and to the unprejudiced eye they signify fertility and endurance through the seasons. As late as the Second World War, in Britain, dandelion roots were used to make a coffee substitute. Rich in iron and vitamins, nettle-tops add zest to vegetable soups or stews.

Late July brings its own summer harvest to the table. This year has brought extra-special family gatherings as the coronavirus need for physical distancing eases, for now at least. Setting out a buffet of homegrown summer salads, alongside fresh fish and eggs, provides both feast and celebration. Salad leaves, onions, radish, beetroot and white turnip. Potatoes with parsley, coleslaw cabbage and carrot, mint, fennel, dill and oregano. Strawberries, raspberries and blackberries abound.

As the feast ends, the heavens open for a thunderous soaking of the earth. It is another form of blessing. Yet, even as summer seems at its Scottish peak, the growth surge is slowing. Second cropping becomes harder. We begin July chanting with Dylan Thomas that 'the force that through the green fuse drives the flower/drives my green age'. We want, however, to avoid for now his follow-on that this same force 'that blasts the roots of trees is my destroyer'.

Let us enjoy each season for what it brings, in its own time, and resist the blights of melancholy foresight or regret. In the apt words of poet e.e. cummings:

rosetree, rosetree,
you're a song to see: whose
all (you're a sight to sing)
poems are opening
as if an earth was but
playing at birthdays.

Jack and the Magic Beans

Once upon a time, a woman had a single son named Jack, and a cow named Milky Coo. And all they had to live on was the milk the cow gave every morning, which Jack carried to the market and sold. But one summer morning, Milky Coo was dry and they didn't know what to do.

'What shall we do, what shall we do?' said the mother, wringing her hands.

'Cheer up, mother, I'll go and get work somewhere,' said Jack.

'We've tried that before, and nobody would take you on,' said his mother. 'We must sell Milky Coo and do something with the money.'

'All right,' said Jack. 'It's market-day – I'll soon sell Milky Coo.'

So, he took the cow's rope in his hand, and off he started. He hadn't gone far when he met a funny-looking old man, who said to him, 'Morning, Jack.'

'Good morning to you,' said Jack, wondering how the stranger knew his name.

'Where are you off to? asked the old man.

'I'm going to market to sell our cow.'

'And you look the right kind of lad to sell cows,' said the man. 'I wonder if you know how many beans make five.'

'Two in each hand and one in your mouth,' said Jack, sharp as a needle.

'Right,' said the man. 'And here they are,' he went on, pulling some large, red beans out of his pocket. 'As you're so sharp, I don't mind swapping with you – your cow for these beans.'

'What?' said Jack.

'Ah! You don't know what these beans are,' said the man. 'If you plant them in the garden overnight, by morning they grow right up to the sky.'

'Really!' said Jack.

'Yes, and if that isn't true, you can have your cow back.'

'Right-o,' said Jack, and handed over Milky Coo's rope, pocketing the beans.

Back home went Jack, and as he hadn't gone very far, it was early when he got to his door.

'Back already?' said his mother, 'How much did you get for Milky Coo?'

'You'll never guess, mother,' said Jack.

'Good boy! Five pounds, ten, fifteen? No, it can't be twenty?'

'You can't guess – I told you. I got these magical beans; plant them overnight and …'

'What?' said Jack's mother. 'You've given away my Milky Coo, best milker in the land, for a handful of beans? Take that! And that! And as for your precious beans, here they go out of the window. And now off to bed you go, without sup of food or drop of drink.'

And the poor woman sat down and wept.

Jack went upstairs to his little room in the attic, and sad and sorry he was, for the loss of his supper and for his mother's sake. At last, he dropped off to sleep.

When he woke up, the room looked funny. The sun was shining into part of it, and yet all the rest was quite dark and shady. So, Jack jumped up and went to the window. And what do you think he saw? Why, the beans his mother had thrown out of the window into the garden, had sprung up into a giant beanstalk that went up and up and up till it reached the sky. So, the old man spoke truth after all.

The beanstalk grew quite close past Jack's window, and all he had to do was to give a jump on to the beanstalk, which was made like a big, plaited ladder. So, Jack climbed, and he climbed, and he climbed, and he climbed, and he climbed, till, at last, he reached the sky.

And when he got there, he found a long, broad road going as straight as a dart. He walked along, and he walked along, and he walked along, till he came to a great, big, tall house, and on the doorstep there was a great, big, tall woman.

'Good morning, mam,' said Jack, polite-like. 'Could you be so kind as to give me some breakfast?' After all, he hadn't had anything to eat the night before and was as hungry as a hunter.

'Breakfast you want, is it?' said the great, big, tall woman. 'It's breakfast you'll be if you don't move off from here. My man is the Ogre and there's nothing he likes better than fried boy on toast. You'd better be moving on for he'll soon be coming.'

'Oh! Please mam, give me something to eat. I've had nothing since yesterday morning, really and truly,' said Jack. 'I'll die of hunger anyway.'

Well, the Ogre's wife wasn't such a bad sort. She took Jack into the kitchen and gave him a chunk of bread and a jug of milk. But Jack hadn't half-finished these when – thump! thump! thump! – the whole house began to tremble with the noise of someone coming. Someone large.

'Goodness gracious me! It's my old man,' said the Ogre's wife. 'What on earth shall I do? Here, come quick and jump in here.' And she bundled Jack into the oven just as the Ogre came in.

And he was a big one. He had three cows strung up by the heels on his belt, and he unhooked them and threw them down on the table. 'Here, wife, toast me a couple of these for breakfast. Ah, what's this I smell?

Fee-fi-fo-fum,
I smell the blood of an Englishman,
Be he alive, or be he dead
I'll have his bones to grind my bread.

'Nonsense, dear,' said his wife. 'You're dreaming. Or perhaps you smell the scraps of that little boy you liked so much for yesterday's dinner. Here, go and have a wash and tidy up, and by the time you come back your breakfast will be ready for you.'

So, the Ogre went off, and Jack was just going to jump out of the oven and run off when the woman stopped him. 'Wait till he's asleep; he always has a snooze after breakfast.'

Well, the Ogre had his breakfast, and after that he went to a big chest and took out of it a few bags of gold and sat down counting them till at last his head began to nod and he snored till the whole house shook. Jack crept out on tiptoe from his oven, and as he was passing the Ogre, he took one of the bags of gold under his arm, and off he peltered, till he came to the beanstalk, and then he threw down the bag of gold, which of course fell into his mother's garden, and then he climbed down, and climbed down, till at last he got home and told his mother.

And Jack showed her the gold. 'Well, mother, wasn't I right about the beans. They are really magical.'

So, they lived on the bag of gold for some time, but at last they came to the end of that, so Jack made up his mind to try his luck once more up at the top of the beanstalk. One fine morning, he got up early and got on to the beanstalk, and he climbed, and he climbed, and he climbed, and he climbed, till at last he got on the road again and came to the big, tall house he had been to before. There, sure enough, was the big, tall woman a-standing on the doorstep.

'Good morning, mam,' said Jack, as bold as brass. 'Could you be so good as to give me something to eat?'

'Go away, my boy,' said the big, tall woman, 'or else my man will eat you up for breakfast. But aren't you the lad who came here once before? That very day, my Ogre missed one of his bags of gold.'

'That's strange, mam,' said Jack. 'Dare say I could tell you something about that but I'm so hungry I can't speak till I've had something to eat.'

Well, the big, tall woman was so nosey that she took Jack in and gave him something to eat. But he had hardly begun munching, when – thump! thump! thump! – they heard the giant's footsteps, and his wife hid Jack away in the oven.

In came the Ogre, saying, 'Fee-fi-fo-fum!' and had his breakfast of three boiled pigs.

'Wife, bring me the hen that lays the golden eggs.'

She brought it, and the Ogre said, 'Lay.' And it laid an egg all of gold. And then the Ogre began to nod his head and to snore till the house shook.

Jack crept out of the oven on tiptoe and caught hold of the golden hen and was off before you could say 'pig in a poke'. But this time, the hen gave a cackle that woke the Ogre, and just as Jack got out of the house he heard him calling, 'Wife! Wife! What have you done with my golden hen?'

'Why, my dear …' said his wife.

But that was all Jack heard, for he rushed off to the beanstalk and began to slide down like greased lightning.

'Fee-fi-fo-fum! I smell the blood of an Englishman!' cried out the Ogre; 'I smell him, wife! I smell him!'

Jack slid as fast as he could with the hen under one arm, but the Ogre came rushing after. The hen squawked, 'Master! Master!' and the Ogre swung himself down on to the beanstalk, which shook with his weight. Down climbed Jack, and after him clambered the Ogre.

By this time, Jack had climbed down, and climbed down, and climbed down, till he was very nearly home. So, he called out, 'Mother! Mother! Bring me an axe! Bring me an axe!'

And his mother came rushing out with the axe in her hand, but when she came to the beanstalk she stood stock still with fright, for she saw the Ogre appearing below the clouds.

Jack jumped down and got hold of the axe and gave a chop at the beanstalk, which cut it in two. The Ogre felt the beanstalk quiver and then shake, so he stopped to look below. Then Jack gave another chop with the axe, and the beanstalk was cut in two again and began to topple. The Ogre fell to the ground and broke the crown of his head, and the beanstalk came toppling after.

Then Jack showed his mother the wonderful hen and said, 'Lay' to it, and it laid a golden egg every time he said it. And what with the bag of gold and selling the golden eggs, Jack and his mother became very rich, and they lived happily ever after.

Fruit of Love

It was a lovely summer day in Eden, and everything was – well – paradisial.

Then Adam and Eve fell out.

It was one of those quarrels that begins quite lackadaisically but rapidly escalates out of control. Neither Adam nor his beloved Eve could recall how it began, but soon the trickle had become a raging torrent.

'That's it!' stormed Eve. 'I'm not hanging around here to be insulted, I'm off!'

'That's great!' shouted Adam. 'Don't hurry back. Life on planet earth starts today!'

And he did, in truth, have quite an enjoyable afternoon, swanning around and picking fruit.

But as evening came on and twilight thickened, Adam realised he would have to make his own dinner – and he had never actually done that before. 'No doubt she'll be crawling back soon anyway,' thought the first man.

But the first woman did not reappear – to cook, make their bed or anything else in that line.

Now, it was a habit of the Creator to go walking in his garden in the evening and enjoy everything he had created. And this evening was no exception. Until, that is, he came upon Adam.

'What's wrong, Adam?' he enquired with his perceptive gift of empathy.

'Nothing's wrong. Well, at least, nothing … '

'What is it, Adam? Where's Eve?'

'She's not here.'

'I can see Eve is not here, Adam. Where is she?'

'Gone.'

'Gone?'

'We had a quarrel.'

'And she left.'

'Yes.'

'This won't do, Adam. I have a plan.'

'Yes, God.'

'It involves pro-creation.'

'Yes, God.'

'Which requires, before gene therapy, and this is before gene therapy, a woman and a man. In fact, the first man and the first woman. Male and female he made them!' Despite the cool of the evening, the Creator was becoming quite heated.

'So, get after her Adam, and bring her back.'

'Yes, God,' replied Adam, immediately, while wondering what gene therapy was, and how he was ever going to catch up with Eve.

Nonetheless, he started out in the right direction, as men sometimes do. But Eve had a head start and she was super fit. The faster Adam pursued her, the more distance Eve gained on her erstwhile partner.

Adam plunged into a deep lake, but Eve was already emerging on the far shore.

Gamely, Adam scrabbled up a cliff, but Eve had already vaulted over the summit.

Scratched and whiplashed, Adam struggled through a forest, but Eve was swerving between the trees in superfast time.

The Creator watched, incredulous at the inequalities that had slipped between his fingers. But Plan A depended on some little humans, which required physical contact. What could he do?

But there was a Gardener in the creative mind, and suddenly a smile spread across Creator's kindly features. 'Of course,' he chuckled. 'I knew I had something up my green sleeve.'

When Adam, exhausted and bedraggled, finally caught up with Eve, she was lying in a flowery meadow. Sinuous and chilled, she was surrounded by little plants whose white flowers were transforming second by second into small fruits.

'Hi, Adam,' she cooed, between mouthfuls. 'What kept you?'

'Well, as you may recall,' scolded Adam, surveying his chastened flesh, 'you got yourself lost, and I've been trying to find you!'

'Well, I'm found now,' soothed Eve. 'Try this luscious little fruit.'

So, Adam sank down in the meadow beside his partner, and the first woman popped the first strawberries into the first man's mouth. Every aggravation had faded from her mind.

'Wow!' exhaled Adam in astonishment at the soft, sweet sensation. But before he could post an extended review, Eve slipped three more strawberries into his mouth and then sealed her gift with a loving, lingering kiss.

Which is why, to this day, strawberries are the fruit of love, and one of the Creator's first wise innovations beyond the boundaries of Eden. As for that pristine Gardener, he breathed a sigh of relief, which may have been slightly premature. It was a first indication that these humans might not prove as trouble free as originally planned. But, for now at least, all anxieties had been dissolved in the sweet juices of the strawberry.

Beauty and the Rose

There was once a rich merchant, who had three daughters. His daughters were extremely handsome, especially the youngest. When she was little, everybody admired her, and called her 'little Beauty', which made her sisters very jealous.

The youngest, as she was lovely, was also nicer than her sisters. The two eldest had a great deal of pride, because they were rich. They gave themselves airs, and would not visit other merchants' daughters, nor keep company with any but persons of quality. They went out every day to parties of pleasure, balls, plays, concerts and so forth, and they laughed at their youngest sister, because she spent the greatest part of her time reading books.

As they had great fortunes, several eminent merchants made advances to them, but the two eldest said they would never marry, unless they could meet with a duke, or an earl at the least. Beauty very civilly thanked those who courted her and told them she was too young to marry, choosing to stay with her father a few years longer.

Suddenly, the merchant lost his whole fortune, apart from a small house at a great distance from town, and told his children, with tears in his eyes, that they must go there and work for their living. The two eldest answered that they would not leave the town, for they had several admirers who they were sure would be glad to have them, though they had no fortune. But the good ladies were mistaken, for their lovers slighted and forsook them in their poverty.

But Beauty was such a sweet-tempered girl, who spoke so kindly to everyone, and several gentlemen would have married her, though they knew she had not a penny. But she told them she could not think of leaving her poor father in his misfortunes and was determined to go with him into the country to comfort and attend him.

When they came to their country house, Beauty rose at four in the morning and hurried to clean the house and make dinner ready for the family. In the beginning, she found it difficult, for she had not been used to work as a servant, but in less than two months she grew stronger and healthier than ever.

After she had done her work in the house, she kept a lovely garden outside, read or sang while she spun.

By contrast, her two sisters did not know how to spend their time. They got up at ten, and did nothing but saunter about the whole day, lamenting the loss of their fine clothes and acquaintances. 'Look at our youngest sister,' said they. 'What a poor, stupid creature she is, to be contented with such a dismal situation.'

The family had lived for about a year in the country when the merchant received a note that a cargo of his goods had safely arrived. When the two eldest daughters saw their father ready to set out, they begged him to buy them new gowns, headdresses, ribbons and all manner of trifles.

'What will you have, Beauty?' asked her father.

'Bring me a rose,' she answered, 'for none grows in the gardens here.'

The good man went on his journey, but when he arrived the merchants went to law about the cargo, and after a great deal of trouble, he came back as poor as before.

He was within thirty miles of his own house, thinking about the pleasure of seeing his children again, when in a large forest he lost himself. It rained and snowed terribly. The wind was so high that it threw him twice off his horse, and with night coming on, he began to fear being starved to death or else devoured by the wolves whom he heard howling.

Suddenly, looking through a long walk of trees, he saw a distant light, and going on a little farther, perceived it came from a palace illuminated from top to bottom and surrounded by a large ornamental garden with a lake at its centre. The merchant hastened to the palace but was surprised to find no one in the outer courts or garden. His horse followed him and, seeing a large stable open, went in and, finding both hay and oats, the famished beast fell to eating.

The merchant tied him up to the manger and walked towards the house, where he saw no one. Entering a large hall, he found a good fire and a table plentifully set out. As he was wet through with the rain and snow, he drew near the fire to dry himself. 'I hope,' said he, 'the master of the house, or his servants will excuse the liberty I take; I suppose it will not be long before some of them appear.'

He waited until the clocks struck eleven, and still nobody came. At last, he was so hungry that he took a chicken, and ate it in two mouthfuls, trembling all the while. After this, he drank a few glasses of wine and, growing more courageous, he went out of the hall, and crossed through several grand apartments with magnificent furniture, until he came into a chamber with a very comfortable bed. As he was exhausted and it was past midnight, he shut the door and went to bed.

It was ten the next morning before the merchant awoke, and as he was going to rise, he was astonished to see a new suit of clothes beside his bed. 'This palace belongs to some kind fairy,' he thought, 'who has seen and pitied my distress'. He looked through a window, but instead of snow saw rose trees and delightful arbours, interwoven with the most beautiful flowers he had ever seen.

He returned to the great hall and found some hot chocolate ready-made on a little table. 'Thank you, Good Fairy,' said he aloud, 'for being so generous; I am extremely obliged for all your favours.'

The good man drank his chocolate and then went to look for his horse. Passing through an arbour of roses, he remembered Beauty's request. He broke off a branch on which several exquisite blooms flowered. Immediately he heard a great noise and saw such a fearful Beast coming towards him that he was ready to faint away.

'You ingrate!' said the Beast, in a terrible voice. 'I have saved your life by receiving you into my castle, and, in return, you steal my roses, which I value more than anything in the universe. You shall die for it; I give you one quarter of an hour to prepare yourself.'

The merchant fell on his knees and lifted both his hands, 'My Lord,' said he. 'I beg you to forgive me. I had no intention to offend in gathering roses for one of my daughters, who desired me to bring her this flower.'

'My name is not Lord,' replied the monster, 'but Beast. I like people to speak as they think, so do not imagine I am moved by any of your flattering speeches. But you say you have daughters? I will forgive you if one of them comes willingly, and suffers in your place. No more words; go about your business. But swear that if your daughters refuse to die in your stead, you will return within three months.'

The merchant had no mind to sacrifice his daughters to the ugly monster, but he thought, with this respite, he would see them once more, so he promised under oath he would return. And the Beast told him he might set out when he pleased, but added, 'You may not depart empty-handed; go back to the room where you slept, and you will see a chest; fill it with whatever you like best, and I will send it to your home.' With these words, the Beast withdrew.

'Well,' said the good man to himself. 'If I must die, I shall have the comfort of leaving something to my poor children.' He returned to the bedchamber, and finding a quantity of pieces of gold, he filled the chest the Beast had mentioned, locked it, and took his horse out of the stable, leaving the palace with as much grief as he had entered it with joy. The horse, of her own accord, took one of the roads through the forest, and in a few hours the good man was at home.

His children came round him, but instead of receiving their embraces with pleasure, he looked on them, and holding up the branch he had in his hands, he burst into tears. 'Here, Beauty, take these roses, for little do you know how dear they are like to cost your unhappy father.' Then he related his fatal adventure. Immediately the two eldest put up lamentable outcries, and said all manner of ill-natured things to Beauty, who did not cry at all.

'See the pride of that little wretch,' they said. 'She would not ask for fine clothes, as we did. No, Miss Beauty wanted to distinguish herself, so now she will be the death of our poor father. Yet she does not so much as shed a tear.'

'Why should I weep?' answered Beauty. 'For my father will not suffer on my account. I will deliver myself up to the monster in all his fury. My death will be a proof of my tender love for him.'

'Do not imagine any such thing,' said the merchant. 'Your offer is kind and generous, but I cannot yield to it. I am old, and have not long to live, so can only lose a few years, which I regret for your sakes alone, my dear children.'

'You shall not go to the palace without me,' said Beauty. 'You cannot stop me from following you.'

All they could say was to no purpose. Beauty still insisted on setting out for the fine palace. Her sisters were delighted, for her love made them bitter.

The horse took the direct road to the palace, and towards evening they saw it illuminated as before. The horse went off into the stable and the good man and his daughter came into the great hall, where they found a table splendidly laid with two covers. The merchant had no heart to eat, but Beauty, endeavouring to appear cheerful, sat down to the table and helped him. 'This Beast,' she thought, 'surely has a mind to fatten me before he eats me, since he provides such plentiful entertainment.'

After supper they heard a loud noise, and the merchant, all in tears, bid his poor child farewell, for he thought Beast was coming. Beauty was terrified at Beast's horrid form, but she took courage as well as she could and, the monster having asked her if she came willingly, she said, trembling but firmly, 'Yes'.

'You are very good, and I am greatly obliged to you. Honest man, go your ways tomorrow morning, but never think of coming here again.' And immediately the monster withdrew.

'Oh, daughter,' said the merchant, embracing Beauty. 'I am almost frightened to death, please go back, and let me stay here.'

'No, Father,' said Beauty. 'You will set out tomorrow morning and leave me to the care and protection of providence.'

They went to bed, thinking they should not close their eyes all night but as soon as they lay down, they fell fast asleep.

In the morning, the father could not help crying bitterly when he took leave of his dear child. As soon as he was gone, Beauty sat down in the great hall and began crying too but, as she was resolute, she determined not to be uneasy in the little time she had left, for she firmly believed Beast would consume her that night.

However, Beauty thought she might as well walk about and view this fine castle and its beautiful gardens, which she could not help admiring. It was a pleasant place, and she was extremely surprised at seeing a door over which was written, 'Beauty's Apartment'. She opened it and was dazzled with its magnificence but what chiefly took up her attention was a large library, a harpsichord and several music books.

'Well, I see they will not let my time hang heavy upon my hands.' Then she reflected, 'Were I only to stay here a day, there would not have been all these preparations.' This thought inspired her with fresh courage.

At noon she found dinner ready and was entertained at table with an excellent concert of music, though without seeing anybody. But at night, as she was sitting down to supper, she heard the noise Beast made, and could not help being terrified.

'Beauty,' said the monster. 'Will you let me see you sup?'

'That is as you please,' answered Beauty, trembling.

'No,' replied the Beast. 'You alone are mistress here. You need only bid me gone if my presence is troublesome and I will immediately withdraw. But tell me, do not you think me very ugly?'

'That is true,' said Beauty, 'but I believe you are very good natured.'

'So I am,' said the monster, 'but then, besides my ugliness, I have no sense. I know very well that I am a poor, silly, stupid creature.'

'It's not folly to think so,' replied Beauty, 'for no fool ever knew this or had so humble a conceit.'

'Eat then, Beauty,' said the monster, 'and try to amuse yourself here, for everything is yours. I should be very uneasy if you were not happy.'

'You are obliging,' answered Beauty. 'I am touched by your kindness.'

'Yes, yes,' said the Beast. 'My heart is good, but still I am a monster.'

'Many deserve that name, but I prefer you, just as you are, to those whose human form hides treacherous and ungrateful hearts.'

Beauty ate a good supper and had almost conquered her dread of the monster when he said to her, 'Beauty, will you be my wife?'

It was a minute before she dared reply, for she was afraid of making him angry. At last, she said, trembling, 'No, Beast.'

Immediately the poor monster began to sigh, but hissed so horribly that the whole palace echoed. Yet Beauty soon recovered her fright, for Beast said in a mournful voice, 'Then, farewell, Beauty,' and left the room.

When Beauty was alone, she felt compassion for the poor Beast. 'What a pity anything so good natured should be so ugly.'

Beauty spent three months in the palace. Every evening Beast paid her a visit and talked to her during supper, with plain sense, though never with what the world calls wit. Each passing day, Beauty discerned some attractive feature in the monster. Seeing Beast often accustomed her to him, so that, far from dreading his visit, she would look out to see when it would be nine o'clock.

Yet, every night, before she went to bed, the monster always asked her if she would be his wife.

One day, she said to him, 'Beast, you make me very uneasy. I wish I could consent to marry you, but I am too honest to make you believe that will ever happen. I shall always esteem you as a friend; try to be content with this.'

'I must,' said the Beast, 'for, alas, I know too well my own misfortune, but then I love you with very tender affection. However, I ought to think myself happy that you will stay here. Promise never to leave me.'

Beauty blushed at these words. 'I could promise never to leave you, but I have so great a desire to see my father, that I shall fret to death, if you refuse me that.'

'I would rather die myself,' said the monster, 'than give you the least uneasiness. I will send you to your father, you shall remain with him, and poor Beast will die with grief.'

'No,' said Beauty, weeping. 'I love you too well to be the cause of your death. I give you my promise to return in a week.'

'You shall be there tomorrow morning,' said the Beast, 'but remember your promise. You need only lay your ring on a table before you go to bed when you have a mind to come back. Farewell, Beauty.'

Beast sighed, as usual, bidding her good night, and Beauty went to bed distressed at seeing him so afflicted.

When she awoke the next morning, she found herself at her father's. The good man near died with joy to see his dear daughter again. But Beauty's sisters were sickened with envy when they saw her dressed like a princess and more beautiful than ever. Nor could her obliging, affectionate behaviour stifle their jealousy when she told them how happy she was. They went down into the garden to vent it in tears and said one to the other, 'In what way is this little creature better than us, that she should be so much happier?'

'Sister,' said the oldest, 'a thought just strikes my mind. Let us detain her beyond a week, and perhaps this silly monster will be so enraged that he will devour her.'

'Right, sister,' answered the younger, 'we must show her as much kindness as possible.'

After that, they behaved so affectionately that poor Beauty wept for joy. When the week was expired, they cried and tore their hair and seemed so sorry to part with her that she promised to stay a week longer.

In the meantime, Beauty could not help reflecting on the uneasiness she was likely to cause poor Beast, whom she sincerely loved and really longed to see again. The tenth night she spent at her father's, she dreamed she was in the palace garden and she saw Beast stretched out under a rose tree beside the lake. In a dying voice, he reproached her.

Beauty started out of her sleep. 'How could I act so unkindly?' she cried, 'to Beast, who has studied to please me in everything? Is it his fault he is so ugly? He is kind and good, and that is sufficient. Why did I refuse to marry him?'

Beauty rose, put her ring on the table, and then lay down again. Scarcely was she in bed before she fell asleep, and when she awoke the next morning she was overjoyed to find herself in the Beast's palace.

She waited for evening with great impatience, till at last the wished-for hour came. The clock struck nine, yet no Beast appeared. Beauty dreaded that she had been the cause of his death. She ran crying and wringing her hands all about the palace, in despair. Having looked for him everywhere, she recollected her dream and flew to the lake in the garden. There, she found poor Beast stretched out senseless, holding a red rose, and, as she imagined, dead. She threw herself upon him, and finding his heartbeat still, she fetched some water from the lake, and poured it on his head.

Beast opened his eyes, and said to Beauty, 'You forgot your promise, and I was so afflicted for having lost you that I starved myself. Now I have the happiness of seeing you again, I can die satisfied.'

'No, dear Beast,' said Beauty. 'You must not die. Live to be my husband. From this moment, I give you my hand and swear to be none but yours. Alas, I thought I had only friendship for you, but my grief proves I cannot live without you!'

As Beauty spoke these words, she saw the palace sparkle with light and music filled the garden. But nothing could distract her attention. She turned to her dear Beast, for whom she trembled with fear. But imagine her surprise.

Beast was gone and she saw, at her feet, one of the handsomest men ever beheld, who thanked her for having put an end to the curse under which he had so long resembled a Beast.

Though this paragon was worthy of all Beauty's attention, she could not forbear asking where Beast was. 'I am Beast,' said the young man, 'and my heart is unchanged. Please, take my hand in pledge.'

Beauty gave the young man her hand to rise and they went together walking in the garden, where they chose fresh roses, red and white, with which to seal this transmuted love. And when they went into the castle, Beauty was overjoyed to find her prince's family and all his people from whom he had been separated. The people received him with joy. He married Beauty and their happiness was complete.

AUGUST

Augustis a month of plentitude. Nature seems peacefully replete and invites us mere mortals to experience the same state.

Flowers, fruits and vegetables are available for harvest or display. Runner beans continue to multiply. Potatoes are there for the digging. Salad is plentiful and herbs add the scent of mint, basil and oregano. Onions, white turnips and young leeks add pungency to the bouquet. Raspberries and blackberries keep coming, while apples and pears swell with autumn promise.

At long last, after months of coronavirus restrictions, the community garden can reopen its Sunday outdoor market. What a celebration this becomes, with fresh local produce and some from southern climes on display. Christina Rossetti's goblins have the right 'crying of the market' for this special fair day:

> Come buy our market fruits,
> Come buy, come buy:
> Apples and quinces,

Lemons and oranges,
Plump unpecked cherries,
Melons and raspberries,
Bloom-down-cheeked peaches,
Swart-headed mulberries,
Wild free-born cranberries,
Crab-apples, dewberries'
Pine-apples, blackberries,
Apricots, strawberries;-
All ripe together
In summer weather –
Morns that pass by,
Fair eves that fly;
Come buy, come buy:

Our grapes fresh from the vine,
Pomegranates full and fine,
Dates and sharp bullaces,
Rare peaches and greengages,
Damsons and bilberries,
Taste them and try:
Currants and gooseberries,
Bright fire-like barberries,
Figs to fill your mouth,
Citrons from the south,
Sweet to tongue and sound to eye;
Come buy, come buy.

'Goblin Market', Christina Rosetti, 1862.

Underneath this feast of plenty, the weather pendulum seems to have swung into balance. We have enjoyed warm summer days and some heavy spells of rain. The soil is moist yet warm. Watering is minimal, and the weeds seem to have grown as far as their desires reach for now.

There is a sort of stasis in the air, which may be misleading. Take, for example, my statue of Janus in the upper garden. Stone carved by the late Jim King, Janus is almost completely concealed, peering out between ferns and broad-leaved ivy. You forget that this classical god of time is two-faced, one looking back and the other forwards. For now, his backward gaze is invisible.

But, if you look closely, the green ferns are tinged with brown. Beneath the impassive face of stone, time is already moving on. Dawn comes imperceptibly later and darkness noticeably earlier. Summer has passed her prime, while the first hints of autumn show themselves to the wary gardener.

Gardens are places ripe for recall and reflection. Memories rise powerfully into the mind when nature pauses between tasks. Stone carver and painter Jim King was an ex-paratrooper and ex-safebreaker. He fell into art through a pioneering prison experiment and an enlightened new system of parole. I met Jim when he was sculpting in the garden of Edinburgh's Dominican Priory, under the benign supervision of Father Antony Ross. After Jim's early death, I rescued Janus from the Netherbow, now the Scottish Storytelling Centre, in Edinburgh's High Street, when its sculpture court had to be cleared for rebuilding. He broke my car's suspension en route, but fortunately not the axle.

I give myself a shake. It is too soon for memories. As far as I am aware, Janus has not looked back since settling in the terrace I created for him. For now, summer remains ascendant so we should sit out in the garden with a glass of wine. Or, as Andrew Marvell, rather more elegantly urges his coy mistress:

Now therefore, while the youthful hew
Sits on thy skin like morning dew,
And while thy willing Soul transpires
At every pore with instant Fires,
Now let us sport us while we may;

And now like am'rous birds of prey,
Rather at once our Time devour,
Than languish in his slow-chapt pow'r.
Let us roll all our Strength, and all
Our sweetness up into one Ball:
And tear our pleasures with rough strife,
Through the iron gates of Life.
Thus, though we cannot make our Sun
Stand still, yet we will make him run.

In any other summer, without the bane of coronavirus, we would be out of an evening in the town, drinking in the cultural highs and hedonistic dusks of Edinburgh's famous festivals. Instead, having written this, I went out after supper, glass in hand, to watch the swooping, acrobatic bats. Within ten minutes, the darkening skies were lit up by a spectacular display of sheet lightning, accompanied by thunderous noises. Once again, upstaged by nature.

Mr McGregor's Garden

Our gardens are so busy with plants, insects,
and magical creatures of all sorts, that we easily forget
our down-to-earth gardeners. Often the story begins with them,
and that is true of one of the greatest garden storytellers of all,
Beatrix Potter.

As a child, and when a teenager, Beatrix went on long family holidays to Highland Perthshire. Not perhaps the ideal haunt of today's teens, but Beatrix loved it. She became fascinated by the ferns, mosses and fungi that thrived in the moist, mild climate along the River Tay. Of course, it also helped that her prosperous parents came to occupy the lovely Eastwood House on the north side of the river, close to Dunkeld, along with nine acres of gardens and riverside woodland.

But Eastwood House had a gardener, whose cottage, lovingly restored can still be visited. An irrepressibly Scots gardener and, of course, a rebellious, non-compliant youngster are joint movers in Beatrix's most famous story. These characters grow in our imaginations, yet have a root in real life.

The trouble was that Peter Rabbit's own father had been caught raiding Mr McGregor's garden, and he was turned into rabbit pie by Mrs McGregor. So naturally Peter's mummy was adamant that Peter and his sisters, cousins, and whoever else of her rabbit kin was in reach, should at all times avoid McGregor and his unlucky garden.

This story has resonated and grown like a folk tale, taking its own distinctive place in popular culture. That may be because Beatrix Potter vividly evokes this garden of her childhood as a place of unexpected encounters. Suddenly, and shockingly, Peter comes face to face with the dread Mr McGregor – a cautionary bogeyman now real and breathing fire and brimstone!

Then Peter meets the birds, the cat and the old mouse. The garden has become a place of encounter and adventure. That is a magic with which we can all identify. The little boy who silently wakes his father to come and see, because in the dawn sunrise two young stoats are playing happily on the patio beneath his window. The old woman who goes out to close the greenhouse door to find that two roe deer have come into the lower garden. They gaze at her, she at them; till calmly and effortlessly they turn and clear the fence in one flowing movement. And in the darkness, the gleam of a foraging badger's eyes, reflecting a young badger watcher's torch, in a wooded edge.

We want this magic from our gardens now more than ever. We want to rewild and revivify the natural world on which human-kind has wreaked such damage. We need more gateways, more green corridors and fewer walls. We crave less confinement and more roaming.

Yet is Peter Rabbit actually wild? He is clothed like a human child, and when he loses his smart new jacket and shoes, Mr McGregor turns them into a scarecrow – something to frighten away the hungry birds that he sees as a threat. But before the whole tale is done, Peter will sneak back with his cousin Benjamin to retrieve his clothes and shoes. The freedom caught by Beatrix Potter is that of a naughty child ranged against the adult world. The garden is that child's, every child's, space for mischief and play.

Some gardeners do not want children at play any more than they will tolerate rabbits, deer or badgers within their walls. But Beatrix Potter's timeless story restores the balance. She brings us on side with Peter. And there were no second helpings that night of rabbit pie in the gardener's cottage at Eastwood House.

A Bride for Mole

Mole appears to be the most mysterious of our garden creatures. That is because moles, or 'moudiewarts', as they are called in Scotland, rarely appear at all, keeping to their underground tunnels and stores, except for occasional forays in search of slugs on a damp night.

They are almost blind and have no ear flaps to make tunnelling with their powerful front legs easier. Moles prefer undisturbed ground so they are more numerous in pasture and woodland than in gardens. Yet they love a nice spacious lawn, leaving their trademark hills of excavated soil and long runnels where they have moved rapidly between deeper tunnels.

The lawn impact is behind the idea of moles as a pest to be eradicated. For, though moles do eat up to fifty worms each a day, they also aerate and drain the soil. At one time, people made a living as molecatchers, partly by keeping lawns pristine and partly by selling moleskins.

Once, a young lad, who was not the brightest of his mother's brood, left home to seek his fortune. Quickly he struck lucky at a grand mansion whose lawn was studded with molehills.

'Can you catch moles?' asked the master of the house when the lad enquired after work at his door.

'Indeed I can – none better,' replied the boy, proudly.

'Very well,' said the master, 'but mind and give them a severe death so the others leave my lawn alone.'

'I will, I will,' assured the lad, touching his bonnet.

Within a few hours the boy was back at the door of the grand house.

'Finished already?' asked the master.

'Aye,' said the lad.

'I hope you gave them a painful end.'

'Terrible.'

'What did you do?'

'Buried them alive.'

In general, however, moles have a good press, although not as visually appealing as the bright-eyed, moist-nosed hedgehog. Moley in *Wind in the Willows* is an amiable stay-at-home, whose venture into the wild wood is the scariest part of the tale. He is a foil to the more adventurous spirits of Ratty and the irrepressible Toad of Toad Hall.

Once upon a time, though, the King of the Moles decided to branch out by marrying his daughter to the best, the most powerful, the highest being on earth. He summoned all the animals and birds to advise him who was worthy.

'I propose the Sun,' said the Rooster, who crowed about Sun every morning.

'But the Sun rises and then sets low in the sky,' observed Badger, who himself preferred the hours of darkness. In fact, would that not make him a suitable groom, given his spacious palaces underground?

'The Sky seems highest of all,' pronounced Eagle. 'Even I cannot reach its dome.'

The Mole King, who had never left terra firma, was very impressed by this proposal.

'But,' objected Rat, who was a constant moaner, 'the sky is often covered by clouds.'

That was indisputably true.

'Yet the purpose of clouds,' drawled Owl, opening one sleepy eye, 'is only to make Rain. Everyone needs Rain.'

'Mind you,' opined Raven, who also had a reputation for wisdom, 'the Rain those clouds bring fills all the rivers. Perhaps River is the most powerful being on earth. Without River there would be no life on earth at all.'

'But River,' croaked Frog, 'is held by the River Bank, so he cannot be the strongest.'

'Not always …' Raven was ready to argue his case when Rabbit, who was getting bored with the whole thing, tried to conclude the discussion.

'That's it then,' said Rabbit. 'River Bank is the best and must marry Mole's daughter.'

'But, you see,' said Hedgehog, shaking his spines with the effort of thought, 'that can't be true since many creatures, including Mole himself, can tunnel into the River Banks and widen, or even undermine them.'

The King looked out of his bleary eyes in astonishment. 'Well,' he blinked, 'there we are. My daughter must marry a Mole.'

And so she did. And that is why, to this day, the Moles live as they have always lived, tunnelling and eating worms below the ground.

The Butterfly that Stamped

Nothing in a garden seems more fragile or more beautiful than a butterfly. Yet the butterfly is not a lightweight accident, but integral to the garden's connected world of insects, birds and flowers. Modern mathematicians say that a butterfly flapping its wings in China can cause a hurricane in Texas. Wise gardeners have always known this, and none was more wise than

Suleiman-bin-David – King David's son Solomon – as portrayed by Rudyard Kipling in his *Just So Stories*.

Suleiman-bin-Daoud was wise. He understood what the beasts said, what the birds said, what the fishes said, and what the insects said. He understood what the rocks said deep under the earth when they bowed in towards each other and groaned; and he understood what the trees said when they rustled in the middle of the morning. He understood everything, from the bishop on the bench to the hyssop on the wall, and Balkis, his Head Queen, the Most Beautiful Queen Balkis, was nearly as wise as he was.

Suleiman-bin-Daoud was strong. Upon the third finger of the right hand he wore a ring. When he turned it once, Afrits and Djinns came Out of the earth to do whatever he told them. When he turned it twice, Fairies came down from the sky to do whatever he told them; and when he turned it three times, the very great angel Azrael of the Sword came dressed as a water-carrier, and told him the news of the three worlds, – Above – Below – and Here.

And yet Suleiman-bin-Daoud was not proud. He very seldom showed off, and when he did he was sorry for it. Once he tried to feed all the animals in all the world in one day, but when the food was ready an Animal came out of the deep sea and ate it up in three mouthfuls. Suleiman-bin-Daoud was very surprised and said, 'O Animal, who are you?' And the Animal said, 'O King, live for ever! I am the smallest of thirty thousand brothers, and our home is at the bottom of the sea. We heard that you were going to feed all the animals in all the world, and my brothers sent me to ask when dinner would be ready.' Suleiman-bin-Daoud was more surprised than ever and said, 'O Animal, you have eaten all the dinner that I made ready for all the animals in the world.' And the Animal said, 'O King, live for ever, but do you really call that a dinner? Where I come from we each eat twice as much as that between meals.' Then Suleiman-bin-Daoud fell flat on his face and said, 'O Animal! I gave that dinner to show what a great and rich king I was, and not because I really wanted to be kind to the animals. Now I am ashamed, and it serves me right.' Suleiman-bin-Daoud was a really truly wise man, Best Beloved. After that he never forgot that it was silly to show off; and now the real story part of my story begins.

He married ever so many wifes [sic]. He married nine hundred and ninety-nine wives, besides the Most Beautiful Balkis; and they all lived in a great golden palace in the middle of a lovely garden with fountains. He didn't really want nine-hundred and ninety-nine wives, but in those days everybody married ever so many wives, and of course the King had to marry ever so many more just to show that he was the King.

Some of the wives were nice, but some were simply horrid, and the horrid ones quarrelled with the nice ones and made them horrid too, and then they would all quarrel with Suleiman-bin-Daoud, and that was horrid for him. But Balkis the Most Beautiful never quarrelled with Suleiman-bin-Daoud. She loved him too much. She sat in her rooms in the Golden Palace, or walked in the Palace garden, and was truly sorry for him.

Of course if he had chosen to turn his ring on his finger and call up the Djinns and the Afrits they would have magicked all those nine hundred and ninety-nine quarrelsome wives into white mules of the desert or greyhounds or pomegranate seeds; but Suleiman-bin-Daoud thought that that would be showing off. So, when they quarrelled too much, he only walked by himself in one part of the beautiful Palace gardens and wished he had never been born.

One day, when they had quarrelled for three weeks – all nine hundred and ninety-nine wives together – Suleiman-bin-Daoud went out for peace and quiet as usual; and among the orange trees he met Balkis the Most Beautiful, very sorrowful because Suleiman-bin-Daoud was so worried. And she said to him, 'O my

Lord and Light of my Eyes, turn the ring upon your finger and show these Queens of Egypt and Mesopotamia and Persia and China that you are the great and terrible King.' But Suleiman-bin-Daoud shook his head and said, 'O my Lady and Delight of my Life, remember the Animal that came out of the sea and made me ashamed before all the animals in all the world because I showed off. Now, if I showed off before these Queens of Persia and Egypt and Abyssinia and China, merely because they worry me, I might be made even more ashamed than I have been.'

And Balkis the Most Beautiful said, 'O my Lord and Treasure of my Soul, what will you do?'

And Suleiman-bin-Daoud said, 'O my Lady and Content of my Heart, I shall continue to endure my fate at the hands of these nine hundred and ninety-nine Queens who vex me with their continual quarrelling.'

So he went on between the lilies and the loquats and the roses and the cannas and the heavy-scented ginger-plants that grew in the garden, till he came to the great camphor-tree that was called the Camphor Tree of Suleiman-bin-Daoud. But Balkis hid among the tall irises and the spotted bamboos and the red lillies behind the camphor-tree, so as to be near her own true love, Suleiman-bin-Daoud.

Presently two Butterflies flew under the tree, quarrelling.

Suleiman-bin-Daoud heard one say to the other, 'I wonder at your presumption in talking like this to me. Don't you know that if I stamped with my foot all Suleiman-bin-Daoud's Palace and this garden here would immediately vanish in a clap of thunder.'

Then Suleiman-bin-Daoud forgot his nine hundred and ninety-nine bothersome wives, and laughed, till the camphor-tree shook, at the Butterfly's boast. And he held out his finger and said, 'Little man, come here.'

The Butterfly was dreadfully frightened, but he managed to fly up to the hand of Suleiman-bin-Daoud, and clung there, fanning himself. Suleiman-bin-Daoud bent his head and whispered very softly, 'Little man, you know that all your stamping wouldn't bend one blade of grass. What made you tell that awful fib to your wife? – for doubtless she is your wife.'

The Butterfly looked at Suleiman-bin-Daoud and saw the most wise King's eye twinkle like stars on a frosty night, and he picked up his courage with both wings, and he put his head on one side and said, 'O King, live for ever. She is my wife; and you know what wives are like.'

Suleiman-bin-Daoud smiled in his beard and said, 'Yes, I know, little brother.'

'One must keep them in order somehow, said the Butterfly, and she has been quarrelling with me all the morning. I said that to quiet her.'

And Suleiman-bin-Daoud said, 'May it quiet her. Go back to your wife, little brother, and let me hear what you say.'

Back flew the Butterfly to his wife, who was all of a twitter behind a leaf, and she said, 'He heard you! Suleiman-bin-Daoud himself heard you!'

'Heard me!' said the Butterfly. 'Of course he did. I meant him to hear me.'

'And what did he say? Oh, what did he say?'

'Well,' said the Butterfly, fanning himself most importantly, 'between you and me, my dear – of course I don't blame him, because his Palace must have cost a great deal and the oranges are just ripening, – he asked me not to stamp, and I promised I wouldn't.'

'Gracious!' said his wife, and sat quite quiet; but Suleiman-bin-Daoud laughed till the tears ran down his face at the impudence of the bad little Butterfly.

Balkis the Most Beautiful stood up behind the tree among the red lilies and smiled to herself, for she had heard all this talk. She thought, 'If I am wise I can yet save my Lord from the persecutions of these quarrelsome Queens,' and she held out her finger and whispered softly to the Butterfly's Wife, 'Little woman, come here.' Up flew the Butterfly's Wife, very frightened, and clung to Balkis's white hand.

Balkis bent her beautiful head down and whispered, 'Little woman, do you believe what your husband has just said?'

The Butterfly's Wife looked at Balkis, and saw the most beautiful Queen's eyes shining like deep pools with starlight on them, and she picked up her courage with both wings and said, 'O Queen, be lovely for ever. You know what men-folk are like.'

And the Queen Balkis, the Wise Balkis of Sheba, put her hand to her lips to hide a smile and said, 'Little sister, I know.'

'They get angry,' said the Butterfly's Wife, fanning herself quickly, 'over nothing at all, but we must humour them, O Queen. They never mean half they say. If it pleases my husband to believe that I believe he can make Suleiman-bin-Daoud's Palace disappear by stamping his foot, I'm sure I don't care. He'll forget all about it to-morrow.'

'Little sister,' said Balkis, 'you are quite right; but next time he begins to boast, take him at his word. Ask him to stamp, and see what will happen. We know what men-folk are like, don't we? He'll be very much ashamed.'

Away flew the Butterfly's Wife to her husband, and in five minutes they were quarrelling worse than ever.

'Remember!' said the Butterfly. 'Remember what I can do if I stamp my foot.'

'I don't believe you one little bit,' said the Butterfly's Wife. 'I should very much like to see it done. Suppose you stamp now.'

'I promised Suleiman-bin-Daoud that I wouldn't,' said the Butterfly, 'and I don't want to break my promise.'

'It wouldn't matter if you did,' said his wife. 'You couldn't bend a blade of grass with your stamping. I dare you to do it,' she said. Stamp! Stamp! Stamp!'

Suleiman-bin-Daoud, sitting under the camphor-tree, heard every word of this, and he laughed as he had never laughed in his life before. He forgot all about his Queens; he forgot all about the Animal that came out of the sea; he forgot about showing off. He just laughed with joy, and Balkis, on the other side of the tree, smiled because her own true love was so joyful.

Presently the Butterfly, very hot and puffy, came whirling back under the shadow of the camphor-tree and said to Suleiman, 'She wants me to stamp! She wants to see what will happen, O Suleiman-bin-Daoud! You know I can't do it, and now she'll never believe a word I say. She'll laugh at me to the end of my days!'

'No, little brother,' said Suleiman-bin-Daoud, 'she will never laugh at you again,' and he turned the ring on his finger – just for the little Butterfly's sake, not for the sake of showing off, – and, lo and behold, four huge Djinns came out of the earth!

'Slaves,' said Suleiman-bin-Daoud, 'when this gentleman on my finger' (that was where the impudent Butterfly was sitting) 'stamps his left front forefoot you will make my Palace and these gardens disappear in a clap of thunder. When he stamps again you will bring them back carefully.'

'Now, little brother,' he said, 'go back to your wife and stamp all you've a mind to.'

Away flew the Butterfly to his wife, who was crying, 'I dare you to do it! I dare you to do it! Stamp! Stamp now! Stamp!' Balkis saw the four vast Djinns stoop down to the four corners of the gardens with the Palace in the middle, and she clapped her hands softly and said, 'At last Suleiman-bin-Daoud will do for the sake of a Butterfly what he ought to have done long ago for his own sake, and the quarrelsome Queens will be frightened!'

Then the butterfly stamped. The Djinns jerked the Palace and the gardens a thousand miles into the air: there was a most awful thunder-clap, and everything grew inky-black. The Butterfly's Wife fluttered about in the dark, crying, 'Oh, I'll be good! I'm so sorry I spoke. Only bring the gardens back, my dear darling husband, and I'll never contradict again.'

The Butterfly was nearly as frightened as his wife, and Suleiman-bin-Daoud laughed so much that it was several minutes before he found breath enough to whisper to the Butterfly, 'Stamp again, little brother. Give me back my Palace, most great magician.'

'Yes, give him back his Palace,' said the Butterfly's Wife, still flying about in the dark like a moth. 'Give him back his Palace, and don't let's have any more horrid magic.'

'Well, my dear,' said the Butterfly as bravely as he could, 'you see what your nagging has led to. Of course it doesn't make any difference to me – I'm used to this kind of thing – but as a favour to you and to Suleiman-bin-Daoud I don't mind putting things right.'

So he stamped once more, and that instant the Djinns let down the Palace and the gardens, without even a bump. The sun shone on the dark-green orange leaves; the fountains played among the pink Egyptian lilies; the birds went on singing, and the Butterfly's Wife lay on her side under the camphor-tree waggling her wings and panting, 'Oh, I'll be good! I'll be good!'

Suleiman-bin-Daoud could hardly speak for laughing. He leaned back all weak and hiccoughy, and shook his finger at the Butterfly and said, 'O great wizard, what is the sense of returning to me my Palace if at the same time you slay me with mirth!'

Then came a terrible noise, for all the nine hundred and ninety-nine Queens ran out of the Palace shrieking and shouting and calling for their babies. They hurried down the great marble steps below the fountain, one hundred abreast, and the Most Wise Balkis went stately forward to meet them and said, 'What is your trouble, O Queens?'

They stood on the marble steps one hundred abreast and shouted, 'What is our trouble? We were living peacefully in our golden palace, as is our custom, when upon a sudden the Palace disappeared, and we were left sitting in a thick and noisome darkness; and it thundered, and Djinns and Afrits moved about in the darkness! That is our trouble, O Head Queen, and we are most extremely troubled on account of that trouble, for it was a troublesome trouble, unlike any trouble we have known.'

Then Balkis the Most Beautiful Queen – Suleiman-bin-Daoud's Very Best Beloved – Queen that was of Sheba and Sable and the Rivers of the Gold of the South – from the Desert of Zinn to the Towers of Zimbabwe – Balkis, almost as wise as the Most Wise Suleiman-bin-Daoud himself, said, 'It is nothing, O Queens! A

Butterfly has made complaint against his wife because she quarrelled with him, and it has pleased our Lord Suleiman-bin-Daoud to teach her a lesson in low-speaking and humbleness, for that is counted a virtue among the wives of the butterflies.'

Then up and spoke an Egyptian Queen – the daughter of a Pharoah – and she said, 'Our Palace cannot be plucked up by the roots like a leek for the sake of a little insect. No! Suleiman-bin-Daoud must be dead, and what we heard and saw was the earth thundering and darkening at the news.'

Then Balkis beckoned that bold Queen without looking at her, and said to her and to the others, 'Come and see.'

They came down the marble steps, one hundred abreast, and beneath his camphor-tree, still weak with laughing, they saw the Most Wise King Suleiman-bin-Daoud rocking back and forth with a Butterfly on either hand, and they heard him say, 'O wife of my brother in the air, remember after this, to please your husband in all things, lest he be provoked to stamp his foot yet again; for he has said that he is used to this magic, and he is most eminently a great magician– one who steals away the very Palace of Suleirnan-bin-Daoud himself. Go in peace, little folk!' And he kissed them on the wings, and they flew away.

Then all the Queens except Balkis – the Most Beautiful and Splendid Balkis, who stood apart smiling – fell flat on their faces, for they said, 'If these things are done when a Butterfly is displeased with his wife, what shall be done to us who have vexed our King with our loud-speaking and open quarrelling through many days?'

Then they put their veils over their heads, and they put their hands over their mouths, and they tiptoed back to the Palace most mousy-quiet.

Then Balkis – The Most Beautiful and Excellent Balkis – went forward through the red lilies into the shade of the camphor-tree and laid her hand upon Suleiman-bin-Daoud's shoulder and said, 'O my Lord and Treasure of my Soul, rejoice, for we have taught the Queens of Egypt and Ethiopia and Abyssinia and Persia and India and China with a great and a memorable teaching.'

And Suleiman-bin-Daoud, still looking after the Butterflies where they played in the sunlight, said, 'O my Lady and Jewel of my Felicity, when did this happen? For I have been jesting with a Butterfly ever since I came into the garden.' And he told Balkis what he had done.

Balkis – The tender and Most Lovely Balkis – said, 'O my Lord and Regent of my Existence, I hid behind the camphor-tree and saw it all. It was I who told the Butterfly's Wife to ask the Butterfly to stamp, because I hoped that for the sake of the jest my Lord would make some great magic and that the Queens would see it and be frightened.' And she told him what the Queens had said and seen and thought.

Then Suleiman-bin-Daoud rose up from his seat under the camphor-tree, and stretched his arms and rejoiced and said, 'O my Lady and Sweetener of my Days, know that if I had made a magic against my Queens for the sake of pride or anger, as I made that feast for all the animals, I should certainly have been put to shame. But by means of your wisdom I made the magic for the sake of a jest and for the sake of a little Butterfly, and – behold – it has also delivered me from the vexations of my vexatious wives! Tell me, therefore, O my Lady and Heart of my Heart, how did you come to be so wise?' And Balkis the Queen, beautiful and tall, looked up into Suleiman-bin-Daoud's eyes and put her head a little on one side, just like the Butterfly, and said, 'First, O my Lord, because I loved you; and secondly, O my Lord, because I know what women-folk are.'

Then they went up to the Palace and lived happily ever afterwards.

But wasn't it clever of Balkis?

(From *Just So Stories*, Rudyard Kipling, 1902)

SEPTEMBER

Transition into autumn is a segue or graceful decline, rather than a dramatic change. Colours mutate and scents weaken. There are fewer butterflies about, so you begin to notice the moths more, especially as a gradual loss of leaf cover makes the pupae and caterpillars visible. There are more than 2,000 species of moth in Britain and Ireland, and research shows that the supposedly less glamorous moths are energetic pollinators, while the exotic livery of species such as the giant hawkmoth is spectacular, albeit not often viewed in sunlight. Moths are lovers of the dusk and night, which makes them autumnal favourites.

Another seasonal sign is the abundance of feathers lying about the garden. Hark back to that outpouring of song and primal energy in the spring. Many birds, especially non-migrating ones, are in moult, conserving their strength for winter ahead. In the process, younger birds are shedding adolescence in favour of their adult plumage. One discarded feather from the supposedly black-and-white magpie exhibits subtle gradation from turquoise to blue to purple – a peacock in miniature.

Rowan berries are left hanging for now in thick clusters, an insurance against winter scarcity, but most edible fruits are still being harvested. It is the season to be berry. Which reminds me of my long-lost gooseberries. I used to discover them in occasional jaggy encounters on the eastern boundary, near the top of the shrubbery. How old might these plants be and of what use? Out of curiosity and respect for their undoubted age, I spared them from my January clearance. They have branched out and produced swelling tangy goosegogs right into October. Is there a science of garden archaeology? Whatever their age, these berries are full of long-stored energy, defended by the fiercest thorns in the garden.

Gooseberries are also *grozets* in their French guise, 'goosegogs' and even 'goggies'. While Latin offers a standardised language of classification, gardeners still revel in local identity. Blackcurrants are Scots' 'brambles', while in Dorset our Scottish bluebells are 'greggles'. Chestnuts may be 'conkers', 'cheggies' or even 'obly-onkers'. According to Richard Mabey in his *Flora Britannica* treasure chest, a double conker can be a 'cheesecutter', while an unripe nut is a 'water baby' in Yorkshire.

Gardening has been driven by a love of diversity through grafting, cross breeding and the preservation of unusual seed stock. This is not just about the plants but the people. At one time there were over 2,000 varieties of gooseberry in England, with intense rivalries between villages and towns, all aiming to grow the largest fruit. Gooseberry festivals and shows were commonplace. Perhaps my hardy little bushes could come first in the 'seniors' category?

At any rate, change is happening here and now in my garden, though at a leisurely pace. The year is turning but there is time within the cycle to ruminate on the fertile seasons whose fruits we are still enjoying. Again, the supposedly puritan Andrew Marvell captures it all memorably, in 'The Garden', which contains the most famous and oft-quoted phrase about gardens in all of literature:

> Mean while the Mind, from pleasures less,
> Withdraws into its happiness:
> The Mind that Ocean where each kind
> Does streight its own resemblance find;
> Yet it creates, transcending these
> Far other Worlds, and other Seas;
> Annihilating all that's made
> To a green Thought in a green Shade.

> [...]

> How well the skilful Gardner drew
> Of flow'rs and herbs this Dial new;
> Where from above the milder Sun
> Does through a fragrant Zodiack run;
> And, as it works, th' industrious Bee
> Computes its time as well as we.
> How could such sweet and wholsome Hours
> Be reckon'd but with herbs and flow'rs!

Grian and Auld Goggie

Grian is a gardener from the old south, yet his name means 'sunny place' in Gaelic. Perhaps this is a reminder of the long connection between Iberia and the Celtic lands of the north. Grian certainly looks the part. He is a handsome man with flowing locks tied back, twinkling eyes and a generous, now grey-gold beard. We have become good friends.

The stories of Grian the Gardener are many and almost legendary. He believes in the language of nature and has encountered every sort of plant and garden creature in his time. Grian is guided by a loving instinct for all living things.

The Gardener swears he once met a slender fairy with dragonfly wings fluttering anxiously above his azaleas. When asked, she told him she had lost her crown of golden pollen. Grian went down on his hands and knees, parting the leaves and pebbles with his fingertips till he found a tiny effervescent band. He hardly dared touch it in case it fell apart.

'Is this your crown?' he asked the fairy, and she swooped down in delight to retrieve her garland. 'Thank you, thank you!' she cried and before flying away, she placed an exquisitely light kiss on Grian's brow. For days afterwards, he went round with a golden gleam between and in his eyes.

Another time, Grian was wandering in the garden after finishing work, when he came across a gnome digging furiously beside a large mushroom. 'What are you doing?' asked the Gardener.

'Looking for treasure,' grunted the gnome without drawing breath.

'I don't think you'll find any treasure there,' observed Grian. 'There is little wealth as normally understood in my garden.'

'I am not looking for wealth,' insisted the gnome, indignantly.

'Then why are you digging here?' persisted Grian.

'Because I am looking for my own treasure,' exclaimed the gnome, losing patience.

'But why?'

'To feel alive, of course!'

And the Gardener left in silence while the gnome continued shovelling contentedly.

However, the legendary Grian met more than his match when he came to visit us in Scotland. He was rooting about happily in my overgrown shrubbery when he found some low, woody plants with grey-green leaves. 'What are these?' he wondered, feeling his way. 'Aah!' he cried in pain, jabbing his finger on a vicious thorn. Immediately he put thumb to his mouth to suck out the offender.

'You've only yourself to blame,' came a rough voice from the bushes. Grian looked down at a hairy, wee brown face glaring at him from the undergrowth. It was wearing a green cap shoved back on its head.

'Was I disturbing you?' asked Grian, ruefully glancing between his pricked thumb and the ferocious wee face below.

'Of course you were,' barked the wee fellow, peering up at Grian's golden height. 'I've been here for decades, centuries, maybe, in my cantie bield. Till you came along, poking around like some messenger from on high.'

'Who are you?' asked Grian, now thoroughly intrigued.

'Auld Goggie.'

'But what is that? Are you a gnome or brownie or an English boggart?'

'Don't English me, big man. I'm Scottish to my core. Goosegog, are you deaf!'

'You're the gooseberry fairy!'

'Fairy be damned.'

'Didn't gooseberries come here from France – berries in the bird's belly?'

'Frenchie *grozets* be damned. I'm an auld Scots Goosegog, wild as a bramble, and much hairier and prickly.'

'I certainly agree with that,' conceded Grian, who could now see the Goosegog's hairy limbs and gnarled muscles. 'And much thornier,' he added sucking at his thumb again.

'No harm meant,' growled the rough wee fellow, 'but you never know who might be stealing the fruit, birds, squirrels or even hedgehogs. This old shrubbery keeps the humans out, till now anyway.'

'I don't know much about goosegogs,' murmured Grian placatingly, determined to learn something from this sharp encounter. After all, Nature always had some point to her communications.

'Well, I'm sweet and tart, tough and hairy out, but juicy and bursting inside. You can make jam with me, or goosegog sauce with mackerel.'

'Mackerel!'

'Aye, but whole fish, mind, straight from a fresh-caught pail, down there at the harbour. Into a hot pan with them – no gutting or filleting. Only fish like that can stand up to my pith and flavour.'

Grian began to feel quite peckish. Auld Goggie raised his shaggy head and straightened his wrinkled frame with native Scots pride.

'Wee Man,' admired Grian, 'you're proud and tall as a thistle.

'Who can eat thistles?' rebuffed Goggie. 'Forbye a Hieland Coo, an' he's got rubbery lips.' There was tough intelligence in the auld fellow's dark green. 'Well, have you seen enough now?' he demanded of Grian.

'Yes, thank you very kindly,' said the Gardener. '*Muchas gracias*. I won't disturb you again but is there any other advice you can give me before I go?'

'Aye, watch out for that wine. He made it with someone else's goosegogs.'

'Couldn't he find you?'

'Thon idjeet has no idea where to look. He's a gooseberry fool.'

And with that parting shot at me and my garden, Auld Goggie disappeared in a rustle of woody branches and grey-green leaves. As I pointed out to Grian later, that was a kind of backhanded compliment to him as the discerning Mediterranean visitor.

'But have you any gooseberry wine?' asked Grian, not to be diverted.

'That's the crazy thing,' I laughed. 'I have. I made it myself a couple of years back and bottled it. A neighbour gave me the berries. But those bottles have lain forgotten in the cellar. Did you dream my wine?'

'And the fish recipe?'

'Don't worry, we'll try the mackerel you're suddenly so keen on. And here's what you put in the sauce. Add fennel, mustard and honey, this old book says. We've got all the ingredients right here.'

'And now, you've got gooseberries as well. I think I'll leave you to pick them if you don't mind.'

I didn't. In fact, I was amazed to find them hidden away in the borderlands of my own garden. Not a trace did I find of Auld Goggie, but then I am not Grian the Gardener.

It was a fine September evening, and we sat out eating and drinking until the bats came to entertain us and the stars to serenade. The mackerel with goosegog sauce was everything that had been promised, and we had gooseberry fool to follow – no implication. But the wine was beyond belief. So dry as to wring your tongue, so pure as to blow the mind into a night sky.

By the second bottle, Grian and I were unanimous that gardening could pull planet Earth back from the brink of destruction. A grassroots revolution beyond the power of governments and corporations could re-green and rewild the cosmos from below. Toasts were drunk, not least to Auld Goggie.

By the third bottle we were pledged to a worldwide fellowship of gardeners and storytellers. An Earth Stories Collection would harvest the best of indigenous traditions; Earth Storytellers would remake education and culture for a restored planet.

As is the way of these things, the night wound down suddenly and it was time to sleep. I went ahead to guide our path with Grian crooning appreciatively behind. As he swayed past the shrubbery, he raised a final glass to Goggie, inspirer and spirit of the feast.

'*Slainte*!'

'Verra guid,' came a caustic whisper form the undergrowth. 'Just mind and piss straight or ye'll miss the chantie.'

Bird or Beast?

As dark late summer evenings lengthen and the warm air fills with insects, the bats come out earlier to swoop, dive and feast. Few pleasures compare to sitting out in the garden without any artificial light, watching, or at least trying to follow, these elusive supersonic acrobats.

Bats are a very special evolutionary diversion. Their true nature has intrigued Ancient Greek and Native American storytellers alike. Are they birds or beasts?

According to the storytellers, bats themselves revelled in their in-between status, aligning sometimes with animals and at other times with birds, depending on circumstances. This seemed to work well until war broke out between birds and beasts.

At first, the bats refused to take sides, pleading their neutrality. But, as is the way with conflicts, things escalated and the bats had to choose or face being attacked by both parties in the strife.

In the first battle, bats joined the birds, but their new allies were badly beaten. However, the bats hid beneath some logs and joined the animals when they left the scene triumphant.

'Look,' said Hyena, 'didn't those bats fight against us?'

'No, no,' said one of the bats, 'we're not birds. Did you ever see a bird with teeth like ours? We're animals like you.'

So, they let the bats join the animal army.

But soon afterwards, there was another fierce battle, and this time the birds won. So, as the animals fled in panic, the bats hid in some trees. And as the birds flew off in triumph and good order, the bats joined their airborne formation.

Hawk spotted them with his keen eyes, and squawked, 'You fought against us in the battle. You're our enemy!'

'Nonsense,' said the bats. 'Which animal ever had wings? We're birds like you. Of course we are – comrades in wings.'

And so the war went on, with bats continuously changing sides.

Eventually the birds and animals made peace, but one of the big points at the negotiations was what to do about the bats. Both parties to the peace treaty, birds and beasts, agreed that bats should be excluded and forced to live on their own in the dark. And so it continues to this day.

And the moral of this story is that those who play both sides against the middle may be left friendless.

Or is it?

Perhaps the bats had the last laugh. For today, many small birds only survive for a few seasons, while small mammals like the mouse are lucky to live into a second year. Bats, by contrast, who are sometimes called flying mice, may live for thirty years, or in some cases, as much as fifty! So, defying the boundaries and being a combination may have turned out to be one of nature's cleverest inventions.

King of the East, King of the West

Duncan was a force of nature. Blue eyes gleamed from his weathered face, while his strong workman's hands sculpted shapes in the air as he spoke. Duncan lived many lives, raised in a large Traveller family in Argyll, making his own way as an itinerant labourer and working with and dealing in horses. He could turn his hand to almost any outdoor trade on farms, in gardens, in forest and on shore. And everywhere he went, Duncan gathered stories from his own culture and from others, till eventually his own great talent for entertainment and wonder emerged into the wider world.

I often sat at Duncan's knee to drink in his poetry and absorb the emotional connections with which he entwined his listeners. One time, many years ago, I heard Duncan sharing stories in a reconstructed Round House in Redhall Garden.

Redhall is a walled garden by a wooded dell on the banks of Edinburgh's Water of Leith. It is a community garden devoted to mental health and well-being. What story, I wondered might this setting draw out of Duncan?

There were once two neighbouring kingdoms, each with their own king. They were called the King of the East and the King of the West. For many years, there had between enmity and suspicion between these neighbours and sometimes open warfare. But neither could gain the upper hand, so eventually they decided to make peace.

As part of the peace-making, it was agreed that each king would visit the kingdom of the other, year about. For, in truth, they knew very little of anything outside their own realms, which was a main cause of why they had looked on each other with suspicion and ill will for so long.

First, the King of the West went to visit the King of the East. He was most hospitably welcomed and entertained. He was shown over his fellow king's towns and estates, and indeed everything was well ordered and attractive. The King of the West was impressed, but what bowled him over completely was the royal garden.

The King of the East's garden stretched out in vistas from stone-paved balconies which surrounded his palace. There were ornamental waterways orientating the four points of the compass, and on each side of them fountains. Each fountain fell into a stone basin, around which were rectangular borders blooming with every flower imaginable. Cunningly, the water seemed to flow under these beds and feed into channels that continued into symmetrical water features and finally into one of the principal waterways. Swans glided in the canal and peacocks strutted along raised walkways.

'Your garden is breath-taking, my friend,' admired the King of the West. 'You must enjoy walking and sitting here at your leisure.'

'It is my greatest pleasure,' affirmed the King of the East. 'For, sitting in one of the shady alcoves, I can listen to the nearby fountains and forget all affairs of state. Of course, I am looking forward to seeing your garden, my friend, when I visit next year.'

The King of the West appeared thoughtful. He enjoyed the rest of his stay but seemed preoccupied on the journey home. The truth was that his garden was nothing like the showpiece he had just viewed. Close to his castle was a large kitchen garden and beyond that shrubberies and woodland that led to his hunting parks beyond. Burns ran in every direction.

There was an enclosed garden for herbs and flowers into which his queen could stroll, but the gate always swung open in the wind so that animals, domestic and wild, could move about freely between the gardens and parkland. There were birds, small and large, insects of every kind in abundance, frogs, toads, voles, field mice, moles, bats, hedgehogs, foxes, badgers and even sometimes some deer. They could wreak havoc if not quickly bagged for the king's table.

When he arrived home, the King of the West summoned his gardener. He drew out a plan for a new enclosure, with walkways, water features and formal flower beds radiating from the castle on all sides.

The gardener scratched his bonnet in bemusement. 'Where's the kitchen garden?'

The king glared at him.

'Your majesty,' he added.

'The kitchen garden must be hidden behind trees at the back – there. And that's another thing which must change round here. In the eastern kingdom, subjects always say, "your majesty" and doff their bonnets!'

The gardener pulled the bonnet reluctantly from his grizzled hair and scratched. 'Can be done, I suppose.'

'How long?'

'A few months, if there's enough manpower on the job. We'll need horses and carts as well.'

'You've got six months, not a day longer. Our garden must not look inferior when he comes to visit.'

'Who?'

'The King of the East, of course, fool.'

And then it dawned where all this frenetic change was heading. 'He'll have many gardeners in the East … your majesty.'

'As many as are needed. And so will I. Let's get started.'

'There's just one thing though. You need to leave me alone to get on with the job. The walls will go up first and then you're not to come in until its finished.'

'Why?' demanded the King of the West.

'Because I'm the gardener.'

'Very well, but get on with it right away.'

So, the gardener set about building walls, flattening the ground on all sides, and uprooting trees, shrubs and tangled borders. It was a mighty work that went forward day and night, week by week.

Eventually, the new beds and walkways and water features were all in place. Everything was planted out, tidied and swept. The shiny new gates were ready to swing open for the King of the West and his court to inspect the gardener's improvements.

The king led his queen through the gates. There were oohs and aahs of astonishment from all the hangers-on. Indeed, it was a total transformation – orderly, tidy, brightly coloured in neat squares. Paths radiated out lined with miniature box hedges. There were gracious colonnades and benches bedside undisturbed ponds which were mantled with ornamental lilies.

'It is excellent,' pronounced the king.

There were more oohs and aahs from all assembled, except the queen.

'But …' she said, knowing her husband too well.

'But, what?' he chaffed.

'What's wrong, your majesty?' asked his gardener bluntly. 'Is this not what you ordered?'

'It is,' admitted the king, 'it is, but there's something missing. I'm not sure what.'

'The birds and the animals?' prompted the queen.

'That's it!' cried the king, relieved. 'Sound! I can't hear anything apart from water running.'

And it was true. There was no wind blowing through the trees, no chirping of songbirds in the bushes, no squeaking of voles, or hedgehogs rustling leaves. There was no distant barking of foxes, or the cooing of wood doves, no honking of geese or quacking of ducks, no squealing of young rabbits hunted by a weasel. How could there be? It was all so tidy, scraped clean and flat. The bees could not move easily between flowers, the bats had nowhere to roost.

The king appeared thoughtful. He enjoyed the rest of his tour, and then returned to the castle, preoccupied. The queen read the signs and left him alone to brood. He remained indoors and did not return to his new garden. The very next day, he came to a decision and summoned the gardener.

'You have done very well,' he praised the gardener, who was disappointed that the king had not come back to walk in the garden. 'You have given me what I asked for. But I made a mistake.'

'A mistake, your majesty?'

'Yes, I thought that a garden of the East could be transplanted here to the West. But I am wrong. It does not suit our animals and birds, nor the insects. It is pretty to the eye but dead to the ear. It seems, only half-alive. I want to change the garden back to how it was.'

'Your majesty.'

'Are you upset?'

'No, your majesty. For I did what you told me, to the best of my ability, but I didn't like the results either.

'Nor did the queen, though she was very tactful. How long?'

'Six months, if I have enough manpower. And I'll need horses and carts.'

And so it was decreed, the King of the West had his garden returned to its western nature. And he was very pleased with the outcome, and so was the gardener, and the queen, and so, when he finally came, was the King of the East. Because the gardener did make some improvements on the old garden, mending the gates and planting more borders. But the restored garden was even fuller of life, and sound and movement than it had ever been.

And the King of the West and the King of the East grew to respect each other more and more, and to appreciate the differences between their peoples and countries. And they lived in happy harmony with each other and their gardens.

We breathed out in satisfaction. Duncan had chosen instinctively from his well of stories, and he had chosen well. After all, making good choices from many possibilities is what unites the arts of storytelling and gardening.

OCTOBER

Octtober balances with April as a month of multi-coloured display. The palette may be subtler, with ochres,
madder, maroon and bronze, but it is no less appealing
to the practised eye. The first flashes of autumn speckle the trees
with promise.

Convention divides the twelve months into four equal quarters
but that rarely applies in Scotland. Spring is usually concentrated
in one month, April, and autumn is in October. The ancient
Celtic calendar recognises the two most important seasonal
festivals as Beltane, or Mayday, on the first of that month, and
Samhainn, or Halloween, on the last day of October.

At Beltane, life moved outdoors for the summer, while
Samhainn marked the reverse. Also, on these dates respectively,
light and then darkness became predominant. Though the
equinoxes were also celebrated in Celtic and pre-Celtic culture,
this two-fold division of the year resounds more loudly in surviving lore and tradition. Moreover, those shorter, more intense

transitions still match our Scottish experience, caught as we are between north and south.

If April shows off trees transplanted from warmer climes, then the native species come into their own in October. The silver birch is queenly; the Scots pines lordly. Apple trees are still heavy with russet fruits to be harvested as the month goes on, while the weathered leaves curl sturdily on the branch. Oak, elm and the ash survivors are losing their foliage in the parkland and provide rustling entertainment for racing dogs and children.

In the vegetable beds, spinach, late lettuce, beetroot and shallots are enjoying frost-free conditions. Winter crops of kale, turnips and leeks are gaining steadily even as the year falls back. The gifts of our short high summer, like the climbing beans, are done.

At last, I see some outcome from my cutting back and uprooting of ivy early in the year down the long boundary behind the shrubbery. The climbing roses and the small espalier fruit trees are settling in well. One more winter will bring some more long-awaited rewards. Quick gains in gardening are usually short-lived. Hopefully, these youngsters will weather any frosts this year and bear flowers and fruit for many seasons to come.

In the shrubbery itself, some winter colours are already showing. The acer's green leaves have yellowed imperceptibly. The viburnum's small white flowers are opening and even winter jasmine is on the cusp. These will become winter consolations.

I should be tidying up the herbaceous border, but it seems a shame to clear too soon. Anyway, the stubbornly persistent weeds, inherited from long neglect by previous occupants, have slowed. The grass may need only one more mowing. There is no urgency to be digging.

So, there is time to wander beyond my walls into the parkland, and through coppices and shelter belts of trees. The brambles are still blackening. Though folk wisdom favours early berries on the tips, these latecomers are still packed with flavour. Some neglected sprays of rosehip remain among the hedgerows. As children, we used to go out to pick them in summer and earn some extra pocket money from the makers of rosehip syrup. The clusters of rowan berries are reddening now but may be with us for weeks to come.

Out and about, the squirrels are actively gathering acorns and hazelnuts for their winter stores. If you sit quietly and patiently you might see a field mouse or shrew about similar business. No doubt weasels, stoats and hawks are on round-the-clock surveillance as these little workers make the best use they can of every hour. Moles and hedgehogs are gorging steadily to increase their body mass, while further afield, the badgers are preparing to spend more time in their setts.

Traditionally, October is a month for pickling and preserving. Like brewing, this is a craft business now, with local producers burgeoning alongside the mass manufacturers. We have become household lazy, although this year's coronavirus troubles may revive some older habits. At any rate, local food production will receive a boost, and this year of plague may draw a limit on our global depredations.

We may hope for a return to gentler ways and an impulse towards rewilding. This mellow autumn may be the harbinger of much-needed change. We have additional need for John Clare's consoling words in autumn:

All nature has a feeling: woods, fields, brooks
Are life eternal: and in silence they
Speak happiness beyond the reach of books;
There's nothing mortal in them; their decay
Is the green life of change; to pass away
And come again in blooms revivified.
Its birth was heaven, eternal is its stay,
And with the sun and moon shall still abide
Beneath their day and night and heaven wide.

Apple Girl

The apple is a magic fruit; it has allure and power. Eating an apple was the source of guilt and sin, or of wisdom, depending on your choice of religious legends. In Celtic mythology, an apple-bearing branch – silver apples of the moon or golden apples of the sun – opens gateways into other worlds.

Apple magic, though, is also earthy. Ruth Tonge, who was in living memory one of England's finest tradition bearers, had plenteous lore of orchards and apples. When the oxen were fed in herb-rich pasture and then turned into the orchard, the ancient, gnarled apple trees of the south-west flourished. If looked after well, pruned and freed from too much mistletoe, then the old trees could yield mature russet fruits in abundance. When the Apple Man was rewarded with a New Year wassail of cider, he responded in kind, from deep in his weathered trunk.

'Ah, that was a good drop. Now, you take a look under this diddicky root of ours, it'll take you to treasure right over there.'

And Apple Man waved his bare branches towards the middle of the orchard, where indeed treasure was found. Which proves that the idea of intelligent root systems connecting well-established trees was well known to the old storytellers.

In Tuscany, peasant storytellers such as Raffaella Dreini, whose stories were collected in Florence in the nineteenth century, knew the apple magic. She tells of the queen who wished with all her heart that she could bear children in the same way as the apple tree bore fruit. She was very sad because she and the king had no children.

It so turned out that the queen gave birth to an apple, redder and more beautiful than anyone had ever seen. And the king placed it in a golden tray in the window.

Now, it happened that a second king, who lived across the street, as people do in Florence, looked over and saw a beautiful young woman, rosy and full as an apple, bathing at the window. When the lovely girl realised that she was being watched, she disappeared back into the apple. But it was too late; the king over the street had fallen madly in love.

He went over to visit and begged the queen to give him the apple on the gold tray in the window.

'But I am that apple's mother,' protested the queen. 'I had to wait for a long time before I had her.'

'I know,' said the neighbouring king, 'and that is why you would honour me by conferring such great favour and friendship on me.'

In the end the king and queen gave way to keep the peace. Their neighbour rushed back home with the apple and took her to his own chamber. There, he laid out everything necessary for a maiden's toilette and discreetly stepped back behind an embroidered hanging.

Sure enough, the beautiful young woman emerged each morning, performed her ablutions and then withdrew without a word back into the apple. The king was devoted but heartsore, and he spent every day secluded in his chamber.

But war broke out and he had to go off to fight, leaving strict instructions with his servant that water and a comb were to be left out each day, but otherwise his room was to be kept locked. 'There is a girl in there,' he told the astonished servant, 'and she will tell me everything that happens.'

Now the king had a stepmother who was very suspicious about what her son was up to in that room! She put a drug into the servant's wine and stole the key. Up and down, she searched without finding any clue to her stepson's strange behaviour. She did wonder, though, about the beautiful solitary apple on the golden tray. Curious, she took out a little dagger and pricked round the apple. Red blood flowed from every puncture she had made in its skin. Terrified, the stepmother fled, returning the keys to the sleeping servant's pocket.

When he eventually awoke, the servant was uneasy and went into the king's room to find it awash with blood. He was horrified and rushed to his aunt, who was a celebrated wise woman, to ask for help.

The aunt mixed up potions for bewitched apples with others for a maiden under spells. She ground them in her mortar with a stone pestle and gave them to her nephew, the servant. He sprinkled the powder over the pierced apple's wounds and, for good measure, prayed to the Virgin Mary.

When he opened his eyes, the apple burst open and out stepped the loveliest young woman the servant had ever seen, though she was patched with bloodstained bandages like a quilt. Devotedly, he nursed her back to health, keeping constant watch on the room and his key.

When the king returned from fighting, the girl was perfectly healed and spoke directly to the young man. 'Your stepmother stabbed me all over with her dagger. But your servant looked after me and nursed me back to health. I am eighteen and was put under a spell. If you like, I will be your bride.'

'Like? Of course I do!' exclaimed the king.

He was overjoyed beyond measure, as were the apple girl's parents. So, after the stepmother had been turned out of the house to beg, a wedding was held, followed by a feast comprising all the fruits of land and sea.

And, as for the newlyweds, they lived happy all their days, and never drank out of a dry cappy.

Home or Away

It has been an action-packed year in our gardens, and some say that the coronavirus lockdown has enabled local wildlife to flourish. We have seen a cornucopia of songbirds, and some very acrobatic squirrels who seem to be able to evade almost any net or hatch to feast on seeds and nuts. Despite my best efforts, a squirrel had first pick from our small cherry tree.

Perhaps, though, there is nothing to match the mating dance of the hedgehog. Hedgehogs have been in decline because of the loss of hedgerows and woodland margins where they flourish. In towns and cities, they must be able to travel by night between gardens in search of a mate – maybe for miles – so less traffic on the roads means more amorous hedgehogs. We should establish safe corridors for our delightful hedgepigs and leave openings between gardens.

Of course, hedgehogs are much faster than you imagine, and they can scale walls and fences, especially in search of love. When a courting couple find each other, the male races after the female with an impressive turn of speed round shrubberies, lawns and ponds. Then he circles round her and they both revolve, then whirl like ballroom dancers till, breaking off, they race round the garden again. This can go on for hours until eventually the female decides to accept her wooer, lies flat and lowers her spines. Otherwise, it could be a prickly sort of love!

Thirty-two days later, four or five helpless little babes are born in a cosy nest of leaves and moss.

Hedgehogs hibernate, but global warming has confused them. Some are inclined to produce a second litter, but those later hedgepigs are unlikely to survive into winter. Sometimes hedgehogs wake up in their hidey holes, go out to stock up on food, and then do not go back to sleep because it is too warm. If you come across a hedgehog in winter, be sure to cover it up again gently to slumber peacefully on.

Hibernation has often been a source of confusion to gardeners. For centuries, many people thought that migrating birds such as swallows or even geese were actually hibernating in hidden parts of Britain's still-wild landscape, which makes this squirrel's incomprehension understandable.

A young squirrel was very puzzled by all the birds flying away in autumn. He had followed the example of other squirrels storing away acorns, beech mast and hazelnuts in a hole in the big sycamore on the edge of a golf course. But he wondered if he, too, ought to be moving away.

'Where are you going?' he asked the gathering birds.

'To a faraway land,' the first chirruped, 'where there is no winter.'

'And the trees do not lose their leaves,' added the second.

'And there is always plenty of fruit, nuts and seeds.'

'Can I go too?' asked the young squirrel.

'Why not?' said the birds. 'Just follow us over the hills till we reach those lands that are forever warm.'

It sounded wonderful, especially as the east winds were beginning to blow into the squirrel's drey, high in an old oak tree.

So the next day, as the next wave of migrants assembled to leave, the squirrel climbed higher and higher in his oak tree to join them.

The birds paid no notice to the agile squirrel, but a kestrel spotted the young creature as he reached the brae upper branches. With a flash of eye and wing, the kestrel swooped to grasp the squirrel in his talons. Then he rose into the air with his prey.

But a squirrel is a heavy weight, even for a kestrel. The bird gained height but more slowly than normal. Perhaps you have seen a hawk mobbed by other birds? This time, the kestrel was spotted by a female falcon. The peregrine dived like a rocket and struck the kestrel a glancing blow. The hawk let go of the squirrel, but the squirrel was no vole or small rabbit, and he fell rapidly. The peregrine swooped like lightning to grasp the squirrel but missed.

It was an amazing sight, because the young squirrel was dropped back onto his own oak tree! And the upper branches broke his fall. He was left shocked but unharmed. The two fierce birds flew off, frustrated, in search of easier prey.

When he had scurried back into the nest and regained his wits, the young squirrel thought to himself, 'Perhaps bird travel is not for me. I shall stay here at home for the winter, and not go away after all.' Then he ate some nuts and curled up for a well-deserved sleep.

Halloween Walking

Can gardens be haunted? That question was in my mind when I went early evening walking in the grounds of Prestonfield House. The gardens you see there today, along with the fine mansion, date back to the seventeenth century and the chutzpah of royal architect Sir William Bruce.

There are terraces with emblematic sculptures and a magnificent avenue up to the house, now a hotel. The once-famous vegetable gardens in which rhubarb was successfully cultivated in Scotland for the first time are now largely under a golf course. The present-day owner, James Thomson, is hospitably welcoming to local people who wander round to admire the resident peacocks and highland cows.

Yet, like the medieval ploughed rigs still visible under the fairways, there are suggestions here of something older and sadder. Gardens harbour the presence of former times. Prestonfield House was once Priestfield House, but its name was changed after anti-Catholic rioters burned down the older house. Priestfield recalled the Cistercian Brothers who once lived here, working the land and cultivating a monastic garden full of healing herbs.

Other troubles linger, and they are also associated with religion. The grounds border onto Duddingston Loch, nestling below Arthur's Seat, and across those evocative waters is the ancient church of Duddingston, once called by the monkish chroniclers of Kelso in old Brythonic, *Tref-yr-Lyn* – the settlement by the lake.

In the early seventeenth century, during fierce religious conflict in Scotland, a brilliant, cavalier clergyman was appointed to Duddingston Kirk by Charles I, in defiance of Presbyterian proprieties. Robert Menteith, who had been educated in France, was discontented with his poor parish of bonded labourers, miners and saltpanners. Soon, he was wooing the aristocratic Hamilton family, then Lairds of Priestfield. This play was successful, and a special gallery or loft was added to the church to accommodate these new upmarket attenders.

In the process, however, the gallant reverend was much taken by young Dame Anna, the lady of the manor, and she to him. Soon, the minister's boat was seen to be frequently crossing the loch, especially when the Laird was unavoidably detained on legal and government business. Some say that messenger pigeons went to and fro between the lovers; others that, in those days, there were fewer trees and a clear view between the Kirk of Duddingston and the tower of Priestfield.

However secret the communications were, a scandal erupted and an 'illicit amour' was cited. Robert Menteith fled to France. There he entered the service of France's greatest statesman, Cardinal Richelieu, and was made a Canon of Notre-Dame.

Charles I, however, refused to pardon the offender for his 'foul adulterie'. Dame Anna was left spurned by respectable society and persecuted by her outraged older husband. She pined alone at Priestfield, walking its ancient garden terraces and sheltering in its arbours. She may be here yet, the Lady of Priestfield.

Amidst this lady's melancholy reflections, a memory rose unbidden in my mind. Fifty years ago, to this very night, I was staying at the ancient manor house of Powis on the Carse of Stirling. Why was I there? Because, as a teenager, I had volunteered to help the community of venerable women who lived in Powis to look after their extensive vegetable gardens.

They had been brought together by common cultural and religious interests after the Second World War and had grown graciously older together. But, for various reasons, they needed to disperse for an autumn break. I was left in sole charge and asked to stay overnight.

Picture an early eighteenth-century classical house with its avenue of trees and a double semicircular stairway in the grand entrance. Everything here had settled, literally, given the later Manor Powis coal workings, into a form of comfortable yet respectable decay. There was one whole wing, though, my favourite, which housed the kitchen and store houses. This was the earlier sixteenth-century manor house, with low ceilings and stone-flagged floors. The extensive gardens lay behind on the flat fertile carselands.

Having skipped end-of-week school, I laboured hard for two whole days, clearing overgrown beds and harvesting late vegetables. I organised simple meals in the old wing and then went to bed. The weather was exceptionally warm and dry for late October. There was no hint of frost, but late autumn mists would creep up from the Forth each evening. My third and last night was 31 October – a Sunday, as it happened.

The mist rolled in early that day, so I finished work promptly. I was very tired and made do with soup and rolls, before going off to watch some TV. Now the Powis House sorority did not wholly approve of television, so their set was tucked away in a small windowless room behind the grand semicircular staircase in the entranceway. There was a matching room on the other side that was a cupboard. The doors were painted out in the wall for the look of it or, some suggested, for concealment in more troubled times.

And that was fifty years ago. I cannot recall what I watched, but I fell asleep in front of the TV. When I came to, the screen was a fuzzy blank. But the air was freezing, as if the river haar had penetrated the house and coiled in this tiny room. I was shivering. But worse, I was gripped by cold fear. Something was in this room. I tore myself out of the chair, pulled the door open and ran for my bed in the old wing, never looking behind. In a short time, though, in the safety of my comfortable bedroom, I was asleep again.

Waking the next morning, I wondered if I had imagined the cold and terror. Maybe I had seen something scary on the television and been dreaming …

The ladies arrived back that day from their holidays and asked me if everything had been fine. I assured them it had, but then mentioned the little room behind the staircase.

'I was watching TV in there last night and something strange happened. I dozed off and then woke up very cold and frightened.'

They looked at each other. 'There's an old story.'

'Yes, that after the Battle of Sherriffmuir, a wounded Jacobite was given refuge here.'

'The Lady of Powis hid him in that room and nursed him back to health.'

'But the redcoats came, dragged him out and bayonetted him before her eyes.'

'She pined and died.'

'The locals say the Lady of Powis goes walking through the gardens.'

'Perhaps you brought her back into this room.'

'Thanks for telling me that.'

'But it is just a story.'

'We're glad everything went well.'

'Yes, we're very grateful.'

I shrugged off the past and turned out of the grand gateway of Prestonfield House. But something made me look back in the gathering gloom up the tree-lined avenue. It was deserted, apart from a luminous wide-winged barn owl beating its solitary way towards the disappearing house.

NOVEMBER

After October's defiant brightness, colour seems to drain away from the garden and the skies. The few remaining leaves seem forlorn. The days shorten, and both morning and evening lose their distinctive forms. Some early touches of frost try to re-establish sharper definition, but as the weeks advance, so do the winds and rain.

The replanted herbaceous border has done well in its first full year, but most things are now dying back. I take the foxgloves, yarrow and lady's mantle back to ground level, but leave the Michaelmas daisies and the anemones with their final foliage. I am not sure if I am choosing correctly in each case, as this is a new venture for me.

Alchemilla is the formal name for lady's mantle, recalling the search for a philosopher's stone that would turn base matter into gold. In the summer, you can see all the colours of the rainbow in the tiny droplets of water that are held between the plant's hairs. But not in November – the stems join their humbler neighbours in the compost heap.

The shrubbery is an easier proposition as it is well established – too well established in some cases. I prune back barberry and forsythia for a second time this year, but not too hard. Their distinctive orange and yellow flowers will be among the first colours of spring.

The rose shrubs need much gentler treatment, especially our Stanwell rose bushes. This is a British hybrid, grown first in the Cambridge Botanical Garden. We planted it in honour of Stanwell Nursery School in Edinburgh where my wife is the headteacher. 'Stane' or 'stone well' – what is in a name? Perhaps the long and much-loved contribution of early years education to generations of local children.

Forsythia is named for William Forsyth, a nineteenth-century plant hunter of mixed reputation. Yet his plant is standard in Edinburgh's respectable suburban gardens.

Beyond the garden wall, the eye is still led over the sloping parkland and fringes of wood to the now bare rocky hump of Arthur's Seat. The landform is always there, but life has lowered its level, withdrawing energy and colour. We can walk over the year's dying.

Yet that may be our imaginative conceit, as romantic humans. Others are more practical. The squirrels are still squirrelling, the jackdaws move daily between town roofs and woodland, and the rabbits are out to feed as normal. There are geese on the move overhead but sometimes these are not long-distance migrants but locals commuting between Duddingston Loch and Blackford Pond, a couple of miles away.

Time to tidy up on the vegetable beds. I have removed the canes to dry and pulled out dead bean plants. There is little to compost, so I heap them up in a tangle. The trees are shedding twigs, so I gather them up as well, along with any dead wood from the shrubbery. I notice that the rooks in the parkland have been doing the same, perhaps repairing their heaped-up nests in the treetops.

If we get four or five dry days, I can make a small bonfire that the grandchildren will enjoy. Early November jars, with its pet-scaring fireworks and unnatural blazes. Much better to let November moulder and enable the gentle clearance of old growth. Let things breathe in and settle down for winter. Nobody needs to be demonised or torched in Nature's commonwealth.

I notice that the community gardens are in the same mellow mood. By the loch side, where Dr Neils' Garden tumbles down the last hundred feet from Arthur's Seat, there is a profusion of uncleared pine cones and walnut shells from the magnificent old tree at the garden gate. A few of these will add fragrance to my November fire, aroma to the embers.

On a late November evening, under a slender moon and early show of stars, we kindle some little flames amidst the twigs. The fire takes light easily, reminding us of the sun, its energy and heat. We shall not forget you through winter's dark days. We will keep a candle lit for your return.

Traveller Soup

The Traveller arrived at the village weary and hungry. He had been on the road since early October, living off the land, but winter had set in early. There had been snow and the ground was frozen. In the places he came through, people were anxious about the length of the freeze ahead and their dwindling stores.

When the Traveller arrived, the main street of the village was deserted. The front yards were empty, and doors shut fast against the late afternoon cold. But the Traveller knew that the real life of this place was behind the houses. Every cottage had a long, narrow stretch of ground, with a kailyard, some pigs and some poultry, stretching down to the river. A common access ran along the river bank, but every plot was jealously guarded and cultivated.

The Traveller cut round to the river path to put up a small bow tent with willow wands and a roll of canvas. Then he built a small fire of sticks and, filling a bronze cauldron from his pack, he set it to heat on the flames.

The village folk were watching from behind their shutters. They knew the Traveller and they wondered what he had found to cook. A stolen hen perhaps, or some last boiling of tatties, scraped from a moulding store. One by one, they crept out of their houses to investigate.

'How are you, good people?' he asked cheerfully as they gathered round in the gloom.

'Times are hard, Traveller,' they replied, doubtfully.

'Aye, friends, never harder. It's a blessing I still have my magic stone.'

'What stone?'

'The one that makes soup, of course. You set the water to boil and then drop in the stone, and in no time, you have a delicious broth to sup.'

'Sorcery and wickedness!' cried the men of the village.

'Nonsense!' scoffed the Traveller. 'Just a small piece of natural magic known to my own people for generations. Many's a winter we've had to thole out on the road. How do you think we've survived so long?'

The people of the village were impressed, despite themselves.

'Have a waft of it cooking,' he suggested to the women of the village.

'You know, Traveller,' one old woman said after sniffing the cauldron, 'that soup would be the better of an onion.'

'Never a truer word spoken,' murmured the Traveller, as the old woman reached into her pinny and produced a wrinkled onion. In a flash of the Traveller's razor-sharp gully, the onion was halved and dropped into the bubbling cauldron.

'That smells even better,' he said.

'You know, Traveller,' said a stout housewife, after sniffing the pot, 'that soup would be the better of a swede.'

'Never a truer word spoken,' murmured the Traveller, and without awaiting a reply the woman went into her plot and, clearing some dead branches, tugged a fine swede out of the sheltered soil. Its purple skin glowed in the firelight. In a flash of the Travellers' gully, the swede was quartered and dropped into the bubbling cauldron.

'That smells much better,' he said. 'My stone is definitely working its magic.'

'You know, Traveller,' said a young woman whose headscarf framed a perfect suntanned oval, 'that soup would be the better of some leeks,' and she sniffed the pot appreciatively.

'Never a truer word spoken,' said the Traveller, striking his knee with the hand that was not stirring the soup with his spirtle. 'But where could leeks be found in this terrible season?'

'Wait a moment,' blushed the young woman. 'I am about to be married and my sweetheart will give me some leek for the soup.'

'Quite right, lass,' approved the Traveller, as she hurried off. 'For my magic stone makes a cauldron of plenty.' And some of the people applauded while others looked on in silent amazement at the smells spreading from the Traveller's bronze pot.

It seemed only a minute before the young woman returned with her sweetheart and a handful of leeks. In a flash of the Traveller's gully, the leeks were chopped and cast into the cauldron. Immediately a fresh aroma filled the growing darkness.

This was the tipping point, as others slipped off to unearth carrots, tatties, a parsnip, kale and even a joint of cured bacon. Everyone now had a stake in making the magic stone work to provide an unrivalled, unprecedented winter broth.

And as the ingredients multiplied, and the Traveller stirred some stories into the mix, the people began to talk and laugh and sing and remember what life had been like before they cowered in their houses regarding every neighbour with suspicion.

The soup was passed round in wooden coggies, and everyone ate till they were full. Ale appeared and even poteen. It was a night to be remembered.

Yet, the next day, few remembered when or how they had broken up the party to fall into deep, restful sleep in their own beds. And when they crept out in the morning, they found the Traveller packed up and ready to take the road once more.

'You mustn't leave!' the people protested.

'No, my work here is done,' laughed the Traveller.

'Don't take the magic stone!' the people pleaded.

'Ah, you have its magic now; the poor stone will be needed elsewhere.'

The people looked at him strangely. 'What do you mean?' they asked.

'When you hold the land and its fruits in common,' smiled the stranger, 'then the magic works without a mere stone.'

And without further ado, the Traveller shouldered his pack and went on his way, whistling cheerfully.

And that is how the first community garden began, working the separate plots together as one, and sharing the produce so that no one went hungry. And the magic of stone soup spread into towns and cities, until people began to dream that the whole Earth might one day be held in common.

The Enormous Turnip

Once upon a time, an old man, and an old woman, a boy, a girl, a dog, a cat and a mouse all lived together in a little old cottage. All round the cottage was a garden with flowers at the front and vegetables at the back and fruit trees at the bottom. For every month in the year, there was something to see and something to eat.

One November, though, it was very cold and the ground was frozen hard. There was not much to see and not much to eat. But there was still a turnip in the vegetable garden.

It was an enormous turnip because the old man had been tending and watering it since the spring, when he grew the vegetable from a tiny seed and then planted out a little green shoot to grow in the earth. The turnip was red and white and bulging, and from the top a huge clump of leaves sprang out in all directions. Of course, the turnip was also as hard as a stone.

'I fear the time has come,' said the old woman.

The old man nodded sadly.

'There is not much left to eat, but when I chop up that turnip and boil it for soup, we will have enough to keep us fed till Christmas.'

'But what will flavour the soup?' asked the old man doubtfully.

'I have some salt left,' she said, 'and the turnip has a strong flavour. I can put in some nettle tops and dandelion roots as well.'

'Alright,' said the old man shaking his head ruefully.

Out he went into the garden. Everything was white with frost and it was very cold. He took hold of the leaves at the top of the turnip and tugged, but it was frozen solid into the ground. So, he fetched a spade and tried to chip at the hard earth around the enormous turnip. Again, he pulled at the top, but the turnip would not budge a single inch.

'You'll have to come and help!' he shouted to the old woman.

She put on her shawl and gloves. As the old man tugged the turnip, she held the old man round his middle and tugged.

But the enormous turnip would not budge a single inch.

'You'll have to come and help!' the old woman shouted to the boy.

He came running to keep warm. As the old man tugged the turnip and the old woman pulled the old man, he held the old woman round her middle and tugged.

But the enormous turnip would not budge a single inch.

'You'll have to come and help!' the boy shouted to the girl.

She came outside hugging herself to keep warm. As the old man tugged the turnip and the old woman pulled the old man, and the boy pulled the old woman, she held the boy round his middle and tugged.

But the enormous turnip would not budge a single inch.

'You'll have to come and help!' shouted the girl to the dog.

And he came running and wagging his tail, thinking it was a game. As the old man tugged the turnip and the old woman pulled the old man, and the boy pulled the old woman, and the girl pulled the boy, the dog put his paws round the boy's middle and tugged.

But the enormous turnip would not budge a single inch.

'You'll have to come and help!' barked the dog to the cat.

And she came mewing and thinking how stupid everyone was except for her. As the old man tugged the turnip and the old woman pulled the old man, and the boy pulled the old woman, and the girl pulled the boy, and the dog pulled the boy, the cat took tight hold of the dog's tail with her front paws and gripped the ground with her back paws and tugged.

But the enormous turnip would not budge a single inch.

The old man and the old woman, the boy and the girl, the cat and the dog, were all out of breath with pulling and tugging. What could they do? The turnip was still stuck fast, and there was no one else left to help.

Then the cat remembered about the wee mouse. She mewed for the mouse to come and help and purred to show she meant him no harm. And the mouse came running and squeaking, for he liked the garden and was not afraid of the cat or the dog. When they saw the mouse, the old man, the old woman, the boy and girl laughed to see such a tiny creature coming to help.

But as the old man tugged the turnip and the old woman pulled the old man, and the boy pulled the old woman, and the girl pulled the boy, and the dog pulled the boy, and the cat pulled the dog, the wee mouse wrapped his tail round the cat's tail, scrabbled with his little sharp claws, and tugged.

Again, the enormous turnip would not budge a single inch. Till suddenly, with a crack and a creak, a scrape and screech, a crunch and a lurch, the enormous turnip shot free. And the old man fell on the old woman, and the old woman fell on the boy, and the boy fell on the girl, who fell on the dog, who fell on the cat, who would have fallen on the mouse if he had not jumped nimbly out of the way.

And they all cheered because the turnip was truly enormous, and it had left a giant hole in the ground, which stayed there till the spring.

Together they rolled the enormous turnip into the cottage for chopping and boiling and cooking with salt, nettle tops and dandelion roots to make the thickest, tastiest soup that the old woman had ever made, and the old man had ever supped. And everyone had their share, though the mouse preferred to gnaw on a lump of raw turnip. No one went hungry and they all looked forward to Christmas.

Evergreen

I always wanted to bring Duncan and Grian together, sitting around an early winter bonfire in my garden, to share stories and experiences. I knew how it would go, because as we fed the flames, and passed round cans of Carlsberg, Duncan's favoured tipple, and a bottomless dram, the talk would turn to trees.

So, at last, after so many comings and goings, they were both here, with a long night ahead. Grian was becoming white-haired now with a beard to match and the warm skin of the south. Duncan was more rugged than ever, and the sleeves of his woollen jersey, pulled up to enjoy the heat, were like a map of

Scotland, inscribed with every outdoor trade. My presence was almost invisible, prompting occasionally from the shadows, and absorbing the *craic* – the flow.

'Where did you get the wood?' asked Duncan, inhaling appreciatively. Things had not been the same for this lifelong smoker since being deprived of fags.

'Fallen branches, hedgerows, and some felled trees that got forgotten. There's blackthorn and whitethorn, birch, oak, some beech and pine.'

'Scavenging. You should have been a Tinker.'

I was reluctant to accept this honorary inclusion, in case it came with one of Duncan's bone-crusher handshakes, or a bear hug.

'Every tree has its own character,' intervened Grian tactfully.

'What's your best trees in Spain, then?'

'Oak, beech, elm, cherry – more than here – along with apples, old pines and young poplars.'

'The big slender ones?'

'Yes, they are fast growing.'

'The Gardener has a saying about that,' came my prompt.

'The poplar and the oak. Apprentice gardeners want everything to happen now. They want to force plants on. So, I show them a young oak with a trunk no more than three handsbreadth, and then a poplar ten times the size.'

'They're the same age,' chuckled Duncan.

'Exactly, so I tell them that, and say, which is better, the poplar or the oak? Of course, the poplar looks better, and can already provide a shelter belt for the garden, but the oak will be long lived and produce hard wood better than any other tree.'

There was a satisfying pause as drinks were sipped and hazelnuts passed round to crack and shell. I waited.

'There was a little robin one time in winter,' said Duncan quietly, almost casually. 'It was a hard winter, and the little bird fell out in the frozen woods and broke her wing.'

First story of the night.

'She needed shelter till the wing would mend. And she asked the oak tree.'

Duncan looked at Grian, who nodded.

'But the oak was very high and mighty. "I am the king of the forest," he said, "I don't have time to protect little birds with broken wings."

'The robin hopped on, dragging her wing, till she came to a spreading beech tree. "Will you give me shelter?" she asked, "I've broken my wing and it is very cold."

'"Indeed, indeed," said the beech, "I'm sorry for your trouble, but I have the broadest canopy in the forest. I have to think about my appearance, and not looking after little birds."

'The robin hopped on, dragging her wing, till she came to a slender birch tree. "Will you give me shelter," she asked, "I've broken my wing and it is very cold."

'"Why come to me?" said the birch, barely looking down. "I'm queen of the forest, tall and gracious. There is no room on my slender branches for birds with broken wings."

'The robin hopped on, dragging her wing. She was very tired now. Eventually, she came upon a small conifer tree which was growing in the shadow of the forest. "Will you give me shelter," she asked, "I've broken my wing and it is very cold."

'"Of course I will, little robin," said the conifer, and he lowered a bending branch for robin to hop up. "You'll be warm there. I have lots of insects for you to eat, and soon you'll be flitting about and chirping merrily. You always cheer us up in the winter."

'And so it turned out. The little robin's wing mended, and she was as good as new, ready for the spring.

'But the fairy at the back of the north wind had seen and heard everything. He was very angry at how the trees of the forest had treated the injured robin. So, he sent fierce winds to blow down leaves and even tear branches from the proud oak tree, the spreading beech, and the disdainful birch. But the lowly conifer he left unharmed. And that is why, to this day, the oak and beech and birch lose their leaves every winter, but the conifer stays evergreen.'

'*Gracias, gracias*, Duncan. To every tree its purpose.'

'And mind the poor tinkers have branches to gather.'

The night had begun well. It became a light to memory, recovering the ghosts of winters past.

DECEMBER

When December arrives, it is still mild with no true feel of winter. But it is wetter, and I am glad I did my wood gathering in November when the sun was more with us. Wood stacking was once taken as a sign of how severe any winter might be – the bigger the pile, the worse the forecast. As winter gathers strength, the life of plants seems more and more to endure in the trees.

Another traditional sign of winter woe is how long rowanberries remain on the trees. As if the birds were saving against worse to come. Our red rowans are disappearing, so the birds are hedging their bets. Rowans trees are plentiful in the wild in Scotland, but many gardens have at least one, which may be a legacy of the belief that they ward off evil spirits in times of trial and adversity.

It is surely true that, for many reasons, trees retain a magical aura, and the most recent science confirms the complexity and resourcefulness of their organic systems – trees of life. They loom large through the winter darkness.

At the lower end of the herbaceous border, the old roses are having a late flowering. These may have been planted by the house's first owners and are tough and overgrown, with gnarling on their thick stems like a stunted tree. Yet those venerable stems blossom into abundant delicate flowers in a display of slow-motion artistry. They begin with a red base and orange petals, but then unfold through yellow to exquisite delicate peach. They have given up on scent in favour of form and colour. So surprising appears this touch of extravagant beauty in the December gloom, as to be a sign. In the language of flowers, the rose signifies love and divine mystery.

December days favour the mosses and lichens. As other plants die back, these underliers of the garden ecology reveal their intricate variety. The lower garden wall is old stone, marking a boundary of the Prestonfield Estate. This is lichen territory through summer heat and winter frost, with a spread of orange, blue-greys and khaki. Normally, they are screened by honeysuckle, a small hawthorn tree and a climbing apple, but all of these are now bare branched.

By contrast, the small brick patio I laid ten years ago is rich with mosses, some light green and tightly clinging, others softer and greener with a fuller growth. These bricks are now happily bedded in moss, yet every brick was garnered from disused works in the local post-industrial landscape, before it was covered over with housing estates, and carries a maker's moulded mark. These are covered over now as if the patio is already an archaeological layer.

I do nothing to discourage those mosses. However, even the sandstone paving I laid two years ago to make a path through the vegetable beds is flecked with moss. Such is the effect of these wetter winters, and in this case, I will have to watch the surfaces do not become slippy. Some scouring with an old-fashioned Scots birch broom – a besom – may be in order.

As the winter vegetables transform gradually into broths and casseroles, I dig over the cleared patches. It seems half-hearted, though, compared to doing a big digging after a spell of frost, so letting the earth rest. Some gardeners eschew digging at this point, but I am too set in old ways – the rhythms of delving and turning.

The rooks keep digging, too. You can set a clock by them coming over from the woods to work any open grassland. They walk forward, each in its patch, and in goes the big beak like a digging stick. Slugs, beetles, grubs and worms beware. Yet, on a closer look, they too are a bit out of routine. Puzzled by the warmish wet, some are still twig gathering as if their nesting season might be about to begin.

Then, sheerly, without forewarning, the thermometer drops fourteen degrees overnight. Those prevailing jet stream westerlies on which our islands depend for temperate conditions have been displaced by a cold north airflow. Suddenly, we have clear skies, stars and Jack Frost with sharp fingers. Now the soil will winter.

On the second day of this unexpected turn, I go over the parkland to Duddingston Loch. Word is that there are already some patches of ice. This is where the winter game of curling was first given organised form. But, as ever, Nature has her mind on other sport.

A migrating flock of waxwings has touched down, resting on the edge of the shelter belt, attracted perhaps by the remaining rowan berries. I count seventeen. Their handsome crests glow in the sunlight, as resplendent in their own passing way as the resident peacocks.

But overhead lurks danger. A peregrine falcon from the crags above the loch has taken notice and is marking out its ground. At one time, old Scots estates kept doves in their dovecotes as winter fare, and these grasslands are still well stocked with wood pigeon and their feral townie cousins. There is nothing a peregrine likes better than to start a meal by tearing the head off a nice fresh pigeon. Fortunately, the waxwings are resting but wary, and they edge into nearby shrubbery. I stand at a careful distance until the peregrine speeds off in a burst of pent-up energy.

By the end of the week the loch is frozen, and where the full burns have overspilled from earlier rain there is treacherous ice on the paths. All things glint and glitter in winter's mirror.

Then, as suddenly as it came, a few days before Christmas the cold retreats north, yielding to unseasonable warmth and melting damps. It seems the fitting close to this unpredictable year of chance and change.

Amidst my Christmas greetings is this 'Winter Wreath' from contemporary poet Ken Cockburn:

> Let me wave you a wreath for your door
> from what's at hand: withies, spruce twigs,
> Spirals of citrus peel, gift-wrap scraps,
>
> cloud-wisps, paper crowns, magpie feathers,
> loops of bramble stem, frayed garden twine,
> a last rose, a line of melody,
>
> the indistinct ghosts of Christmas past,
> everything held more or less in place
> by a clasp as sharp as a new moon.

Donald and Mary

Once, long ago, there was an old couple living in a cottage on the Braes of Glenlivet. They were poor but contented, depending on their kailyard and on the small croft where they were able to keep a cow and grow some oats.

But one year, the winter set in early and hard. The cow refused to milk, the kailyard was under snow, and the well froze so solid that ice had to be broken from its head and melted by the peat fire.

Donald sat by the fire most of each day, cap on his head, getting under Mary's feet as she tried to keep up her routine of cleaning and preparing the soup, which was all they had left to eat. Every so often Donald would howk phlegm and spit into the fire or, pressing a thumb to one nostril, shoot snot into the hearth. 'Can you not take your cap off in the house?' grumbled Mary, 'And for pity's sake, use a rag for your nose.'

And so it went on, the weather remorseless, and the meal kist empty. After a few days, Mary could stand no more. 'Donald, she said, if you don't get out and find us some food, we will have nothing but nettle soup for Christmas.'

'And where will I be finding food in this weather?' replied Donald.

'How am I to know that, you good-for-nothing. Go out and hunt and don't let me see your face, or your snotty neb back inside this door until you have something to show for it.' And she swept her birch besom hard against Donald's boots. 'Men!' she snapped. 'Always going out just to come back in! And nothing to show for it.'

Poor Donald knew when he was beaten and headed out. What could he do?

Being a dutiful fellow, he went in his perplexity to consult the priest.

'Oh,' said the kindly old priest, 'but that's bad, Donald, very bad. Mary's on the warpath. But see here, I have my old gun in the press.

Take that and see if you can take a potshot at a deer on the hill. They must be coming down to the loch. Hasn't been fired for years, mind you, and it needs to be primed with the powder and pushed home with this ramrod. Take the bag for this powder and any game. Don't forget to take the rod out, Donald, before you fire.'

Donald was thankful for this unexpected advice, and most impressed by the priest's ancient musket, for truth to tell, the crofter had never owned or shot a gun in all his born days. 'Surely this will quiet the old woman from her scolding,' he muttered, starting up the snow-covered hillside with a new spring in his step.

Soon, he was over the brow of the hill looking down over the loch, which was frozen over. The snow had stopped falling and the day was clearing. But there was no sign of any deer.

Donald stood and watched and waited. Every so often, he howked into the snow or cleared his nose. He watched and waited, till he began to shiver and lose heart. 'What can I do?' he moaned. 'Old Mary will set about me if I go home empty-handed.'

Then, all of a sudden, the cry of wild duck sounded over the loch and a little formation of three ducks came into view, flying low and looking for water on which to land. 'Jesus, blessed Mary and Joseph!' exclaimed Donald, stuffing in gunpowder with great excitement. 'Would you look at those fine creatures!'

He shoved the ramrod into the barrel as the priest had shown him. 'Just one of those birds could feed us for a week.'

The ducks had come down low. Time was short. Donald raised the musket to his shoulder and pressed back the rusty trigger. There was a loud bang and Donald shot back onto the snow. The ramrod soared upwards, hopelessly out of range. 'Jesus, blessed Mary, and Joseph, forgive me!' Donald wailed, struggling back to his feet in shock.

But as the old crofter gazed skywards into despair, his projectile faltered and then suddenly plummeted, spearing the three ducks right through on its way, and buried its point in the ice.

'Jesus, blessed Mary and Joseph, it's a miracle! God be praised.' Donald turned to pick up his bag and, lo and behold, there was a mountain hare lying there dead, its back broken by Donald's fall. Words failed.

He dropped the hare into his bag and headed out onto the ice.

Imagine Donald's amazement when he reached the ramrod with the three impaled ducks for, peering down, he could see that its point had carried on through the ice and speared a salmon below! He was thinking on his feet now, and quickly pulled out his knife to hack round the ice at the base of his ramrod.

AS

Working fast, Donald hacked and tugged, tugged and hacked, till, without warning, ramrod and jagged ice gave way together. Up they shot, salmon and duck attached, and sliced off Donald's head in one clean cut.

But the old crofter was very fast now on his feet, and swiftly he grabbed the severed head and cap and put it back on his neck. Within seconds, it froze in place. 'Jesus, blessed Mary, and Joseph!' he said. 'But that was a close shave!'

Without further delay, Donald stowed away the three ducks and the salmon in his bag beside the hare and, retrieving the priest's musket, headed home.

Imagine Mary's delight when the old crofter arrived home with his game bag full to bursting. 'Man dear,' she said, 'but you're something byordinar. Just you sit down by the fire and I'll broil a fowl for your supper.'

Well, 'Jesus, blessed Mary, and Joseph', but times were now changed for the better. Donald sat by the fire and Mary passed him a filled pipe. He sat there like royalty, just as he had come ben, and puffed away contentedly as a first duck was plucked and put to cooking. The warmth and sweet aroma filled the cottage.

Every so often, Donald howked and spat phlegm into the fat-spitting flames, or cleared his nose, one thumb-pressed nostril at a time. It had been a rheumy day, right enough. And, between tending the ducks, cleaning the salmon, and gralloching the hare, Mary looked over at Donald, biting her tongue.

'Shall I tell you again, Mary, about the priest's old musket?' said Donald, clearing his throat into the hearth before launching into another embellishment of the tale he could grow old on.

'If you must, Donald,' said Mary patiently. 'But at least take off your bonnet.'

At which, Donald graciously swept off his cap – and along with it came his head, straight into the fire.

The old couple were both left speechless.

And the next Mary heard of the old priest was when he came to arrange Donald's burial.

And the crofter's wake was long remembered for the feast that Mary proudly set out for the mourners, and for the tales just like this one that are still being told on the Braes of Glenlivet.

The Green Knight

Summer in her green robe
Folds in deep dark earth
Pass round the loving cup
And Feast Yule together
Logs burn, crack, crumble,
Embers fire lack hearth
Pass round the loving cup
And Feast Yule together.

It was the midwinter solstice and Arthur kept the Yule Days Feast, according to custom. For, in failing such observance, how could anyone count on the Sun's return?

As that shortest and most perilous day of the year, excepting Samhainn, drew to its eerie close, Arthur was at table with his companions, eating and drinking. Suddenly, the great double doors of the feasting hall crashed open, and an icy blast blew through the warm interior. In stepped a huge warrior leading a green horse. The giant was dressed in green, armoured with green iron, and on his head he wore a helmet of holly boughs. In his free hand he bore a fearsome axe, and round its green haft were bound sprigs of mistletoe.

'Who is Lord here?' the Green Knight demanded.

Everyone was frozen to their seat, but Arthur spoke out loud and clear. 'It is I, Arthur. You are welcome to my round table.'

'Nay,' replied the Knight, 'I have come from the forests of the north, drawn by the fame of this round table, but all I see here are weaklings and cowards.'

A great hubbub arose, and warriors reached for their weapons at this jeering insult. Yet Arthur looked on calmly. He was ever restless at these feasts until some great tale or adventure was begun.

'Who will dare to give me one blow with my own axe?' cried the Green Knight. 'And on Midsummer Day, he will receive my blow in return. I have seen women more manly.'

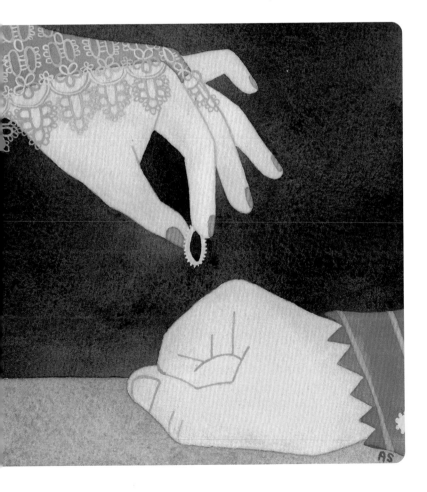

'I accept your challenge,' said Arthur, rising to his feet.

'No!' shouted, Gawain, coming forward. 'That would be a disgrace to your fellowship. I am the least among you all, but I accept the challenge.'

The slight, fair-haired figure advanced. Without hesitation, the giant Knight passed down the axe, swept aside his green hair and lowered his neck. Gawain struck his blow, and the Knight's head fell to the ground bathed in a rush of red blood.

Then the Knight straightened his great frame, took up the head under his arm, and the lips spoke, 'Gawain, I shall await to deliver your blow in the Green Chapel at Midsummer.'

Then he swung into the saddle and his green horse rode out of the feasting hall, leaving the doors swinging emptily behind.

But Arthur called everyone back to feasting. 'Truly,' he said, 'this is a marvel for the sun-giving Feast of Yule.' And he passed the loving cup to Gawain.

The seasons revolved in their course. Bride's spring and Beltane came in turn, and it was time for Gawain to set out on his quest. Far north he journeyed, meeting many adventures on the way, until he entered the wild wood of Caledon.

Midsummer week came, and fires blazed on the surrounding mountains, but still there was no word of a Green Chapel. Gawain slept out in the forest fully armed, his heart heavy with failure. Until, three days before Midsummer, he saw a tower hidden beneath the trees and beyond a mighty fortress.

Gawain was welcomed there as an honoured guest, for the fame of his quest had gone before. The Lord of the Castle, who had a mane of bright red hair and a red beard, insisted that Gawain should stay with them for Midsummer.

The next morning, the Lord made ready for hunting, but implored Gawain to rest in the tower and entertain the Lady of the Castle. Off the Lord went, accompanied by loud horns and the fierce baying of hounds.

So, Gawain rested in his chamber till noon, at which hour the Lady of the Castle came to visit him, to talk of quests, fair loves and ladies. And this Lady, who seemed fairer than Gwynyfawr herself, asked what Gawain might do for her love. And he said he might give anything to her, except the ring on his finger. Which, she said, was little enough.

By and by, the red-maned Lord returned and presented Gawain with a fine deer, and in return, Gawain kissed his host. 'A fair recompense from so honoured a knight,' said the Lord of the wood-girt castle. And that night again they feasted, and the next morning the Lord once again set out to hunt, imploring Gawain to rest and entertain his good lady.

So, Gawain rested in his chamber till noon, at which hour the Lady of the Castle came to visit him and talk of quests, fair loves and ladies. And this Lady, who seemed fairer than Gwynyfawr herself, asked what Gawain might do for her love. And he said he might give anything to her except the ring on his finger, which she said was little enough. Then she drew the ring from her own finger and pressed it on Gawain's.

Skilfully, he defended himself from the Lady's gift, but she kissed him twice and said that Gawain was no true warrior in the court of love and left him alone in his chamber.

By and by, the red-maned Lord returned and presented Gawain with a monstrous wild boar, and in return, Gawain kissed his host twice. 'A fair recompense from so honoured a knight,' said the Lord of the wood-girt castle. And that night again they feasted, with Midsummer songs and rich wines, but Gawain was uneasy and resolved to leave the next morning.

The next morning came and, once more, the Lord set out to hunt with loud horns and the baying of hounds, imploring

Gawain to rest and entertain his good lady. Gawain slept on, remembering too late his resolve to leave the castle that day and free himself from the fervour of the Lady.

At noon, the Lady of the Castle came to visit him, in an open robe, and pressed her love upon Gawain. But he would not yield. Again, she offered him her gold ring, but he would not accept. Finally, she took the green girdle from within her robe. Gawain recoiled in horror.

'Nay,' said she, 'this girdle protects all who possess it from death's lordship. Do not refuse my gift of life.' And, kissing him three times on the mouth, she fled his chamber.

That night the red-maned Lord returned, sad and slow. All their hunting had gained was one thin fox. Yet Gawain greeted the Lord of the Castle with three kisses. That evening, which was Midsummer's Eve, the Lord stayed close by Gawain's side, and gave him directions to the Green Chapel.

The next morning, Gawain rose with the lark, donned his armour and, with it, the green girdle on his sleeve. Then he set out into the forest. The woods sloped downward into a sombre depression where the trees seemed bare, and no birds sang. This was a land of wintry death, even at Midsummer.

Eventually his horse halted in front of a shadowy cave. Gawain dismounted and, as he advanced, the Green Knight emerged from the gloomy recess, bearing his axe bound with sprigs of midwinter mistletoe.

'Gawain,' his harsh voice echoed in the trees. 'You have honoured your pledge. Now receive my blow in recompense.' And Gawain bent his neck beneath the deadly blade. The Green Knight swung the axe, and Gawain flinched.

'No!' cried the Knight, 'Gawain would not flinch. You are some imposter.'

'I am Gawain,' responded the fair, slender knight, 'and sorry I am to lose life at Midsummer, but I am not afraid. Strike and death will be my reward.'

The Green Knight struck again, but the blow glanced off Gawain's neck. A third time he struck, and a mere trickle of red blood dripped onto the forest floor.

'Gawain!' cried the Knight, 'You have betrayed me!' And the giant began to fall down in front of the Green Chapel. And as his great frame crumpled, the green locks turned to red, and his flowing beard became a red mane.

'No, my Lord,' said Gawain, grasping the Lord of the Castle in his arms, for it was his Midsummer host that he held. 'I accepted the gift of the girdle but no love other than what you bestowed.'

'Gawain has proved true,' gasped the Lord, drawing breath again.

Then the Lord began to recover his strength and the bare trees began to leaf and the birds to joyfully sing. And Gawain and the Lord returned together to the castle, where they observed the season of the Sun with solemnity and feasting. And the Lord's wife was there rejoicing in Gawain's faithfulness to his quest.

'From this day,' declared Gawain, 'I shall wear the green girdle on my sleeve as a pledge of honour and a warning.'

The next day, the slender, fair-haired knight began the long journey back to Arthur's fellowship. But that is the tale for another time. The sign of the girdle on Gawain's green sleeve endured until Arthur's round table was no more.

As for the Feast of Yule, it endures whenever the midwinter solstice is honoured. And, to this day, between the seasons of Beltane and Midsummer, the Green Chapel can be found by those who seek their fate in the wild woods of Caledon.

Robin Redbreast and Jenny Wren

When St Stephens Day arrives, across the Celtic lands, bands of mummers or guisers gather to 'hunt the wren'. It is a strange form of ritual merriment in which the wren in some way symbolises the sun, its near death, and then resurrection. It seems unlikely that, in later times, any wren or 'dreolin' was killed. In the Scots version, robin redbreast comes to the rescue to make sure of a happy ending.

In some ways, this is a popular midwinter or 'yule' alternative to the chivalric 'Gawain and the Green Knight'. As folk dramas experience revival, it could still offer a welcome alternative to Boxing Day bargain sales:

> Will ye gang to the wood, says Frozie Toesie
> Will ye gang to the wood, says Johnnie Rednosie
> Will ye gang to the wood, says Wise owl Wullie
> We'll gang to the wood, sang all the Birdies
> Where's the boys will hunt the wren?
> For all we birds are merry men.

The birds or, in Scots, 'burdies' then introduce themselves and show off their finery. Next comes a processional song as they all head out from the village:

> The wren, the wren, the Queen of all birds
> St Stephen's Day wis caught in the furze;
> Although she's but little, her honour is great,
> Jump up, me lads, and gie her a treat.
> Dreolin, dreolin, where's your nest?
> Tis in the bush that I love best;
> It's in the bush, the holly tree,
> Where all the boys do follow me.
> We followed the wren three mile or more,

Three mile or more, three mile or more.
We followed the wren three mile or more,
At five o'clock in the morning.

Up with the kettle and down with the pan,
And gie us a penny tae bury the wren.
I carry a wee box under my arm
A penny or pound will dao it nae harm.

The birds have become the hunting party:

Tao hunt the wren, and free the sun.
Take up your weapons everyone.

[All]
The wren she lies in care's nest,
In care's nest, in care's nest,
The wren she lies in care's nest,
In muckle pain and dule O.

Things are looking ominous for Jenny Wren, but then another
character begins to feature – perhaps a once jilted lover.

[All]
The wren she lies in care's nest
When in cam Robin Redbreast,
When in cam Robin Redbreast
With sugar saps and wine O.

[Robin]
Now, maiden will you taste o this?
Taste o this, taste o this?
Now, maiden will you taste o this?
The sugar saps and wine O.

[Jenny]
Nay, Robin, ne'er a drop
Redbreast, Redbreast,
Nay, Robin, ne'er a drop
Though it were e'er sae fine O.

Robin has been spurned for now and attention switches to the comic business of preparing to kill, dismember and transport a wren, but Robin is determined.

[All]
Sticks and stones will break her bones
Break her bones, break her bones,
Sticks and stones will break her banes
And ding down Jenny Wren O.

[Robin]
And where's the ring I gied you
I gied you, I gied you?
And where's the ring I gied you,
You little cutty Queen O.

[Jenny]
I gave it to a Tomtit
A Tomtit, a Tomtit,
I gave it to a Tomtit
A true sweetheart of mine O.

Now comes Robin's gambit, his quest or adventure to win the king and queen's favour, and then the wren to be his bride.

[Robin]
I'm away to the king
To sing a sang to him
This merry Yule morn,
And play for the king.

Meanwhile, Jenny is left to the mercy of the hunters, who grapple for a piece of the action.

[Cock Sparra]
Look, there she's hiding!

[Frozie]
I'll have a wing!

[Rednosie]
I'll have a breast!

[Cock Sparra]
I'll have the brain!

[Rooster]
I'll have a leg!

[Heron]
I'll have another!

[Goosie]
I'll make a duvet with her feathers!

They make off with their prey.

[All]
Bear her hame
Tao win the sun again!
Eyes for the blind, Legs for the lame
Wings for the cauld, Dogs to the bane.

The wren has been captured, but not slain, and now rescue is at hand.

> [All]
> The wren's true king, o all the birds.
> We've caught the wren, on this Yule day.
> Though she's little, her kin is great.
> We pray you all, give us to eat.
>
> [Robin]
> And to them I did sing,
> This merry Yule morning.
>
> [All]
> And what did you win, Robin?
>
> [Robin]
> The wren to be my Queen.
>
> [All]
> The wren to be his queen!
>
> [Robin]
> Now, maiden will you taste o this?
> Taste o this, taste o this?
> Now, maiden will ye taste o this?
> The sugar saps and wine O.
>
> [Jenny]
> Aye, Robin, gie's a drop
> Gie's a drop, gie's a drop,
> Aye, Robin, gie's a drop
> Because it tastes so fine O.

Jenny is ripe for resurrection, and harmony may be restored between wren and robin, humans and nature.

[Robin]
And where's the ring I gied you
I gied you, I gied you?
And where's the ring I gied you,
You little cutty Queen O.

[Jenny]
Here's the ring you gied me
You gied me, you gied me,
Here's the ring you gied me,
I wear it round my heart O.

[All]
We beat down Jenny Wren
But now she jumps back up again!

The wren, the wren, the Queen of all birds
St Stephen's Day was caught in the furze;
Although she's but little, her honour is great,
Jump up, me lads, and gie her a treat.

My box would speak, gin it had but a tongue,
And two or three guineas would do it no wrong.
Sing holly, sing ivy - sing ivy, sing holly,
A drop just to drink would drown melancholy.

And may we all be united at the close of this gardening year, and
through many years to come.

The Scottish Storytelling Centre is delighted to be associated with the *Folk Tales* series developed by The History Press. Its talented storytellers continue the Scottish tradition, revealing the regional riches of Scotland in these volumes. These include the different environments, languages and cultures encompassed in our big wee country. The Scottish Storytelling Centre provides a base and communications point for the national storytelling network, along with national networks for Traditional Music and Song and Traditions of Dance, all under the umbrella of TRACS (Traditional Arts and Culture Scotland). See www.scottishstorytellingcentre.co.uk for further information. The Traditional Arts community of Scotland is also delighted to be working with all the nations and regions of Great Britain and Ireland through the *Folk Tales* series.

Donald Smith
Director, Tracs
Traditional Arts and Culture Scotland